I0580390

WYLDBLOOD

ISSUE 14 – AUTUMN 2023

Wyldblood Magazine #14 - Autumn 2023

© 2023 Wyldblood Press and contributors.
Print ISBN-978-1-914417-18-4

Publisher: Wyldblood Press, Thicket View, Bakers Lane, Maidenhead SL6 6PX UK. www.wyldblood.com **Editor:** Mark Bilsborough. **Fiction editor** Sandra Baker. **Subscriptions:** 6 issues epub/mobi/pdf delivered to your inbox £20. 6 issue print subscriptions £35. Single issues available worldwide via Amazon and from wyldblood.com/shop

Submissions: we are regularly open for submissions of flash fiction, short stories and novels – check our website for our current status and requirements. We are a paying market. We also need artwork, people to review us, and people to review *for* us. Email contact@wyldblood.com

Issue 15 will be published in March 2024

Editorial

Mark Bilsborough

Welcome to *Wyldblood* 14 – more science fiction and fantasy to warm your winter days. plus a slightly despairing rant about the state of SFF on streaming services (too scattergun, no continuity, extensive season gaps) and some great book reviews (or reviews of great books; whatever).

But first an apology. Last time around we railed against the use (or misuse of ChatGPT and all things AI. So it's with some irony (and a great deal of annoyance) that we discovered that the cover of *Wyldblood* 12 was most likely AI generated. We've replaced the offending item with something most definitely not guided by android hands, but it's been a chastening experience (here's the new cover).

Since then, we almost bought something else that (thankfully, having learned our lesson) we ran through multiple AI checkers. Now we know they're not foolproof, but we're pretty confident we had another close call. We're not an art magazine – we use images to illustrate our stories and because we need covers, but we're here for the words – so in the past we've got most of our images from stock websites where we subscribe for access to thousands of pieces of art, uploaded by real artists. Except, not always, we've discovered.

So we'll be buying our covers direct from artists in the future – we've got some good people in mind, but if you'd like that to be you, send us something we might like. We prefer wraparounds, our covers are 7 by 10 inches and we like strong, bold, uncluttered character based images with a gap at the top for the title – we're not really into horror, either (although we do publish it from time to time). For interiors our preference is simple line drawing or simple monochrome brushwork – for a small illustration at the top of the story. When we find someone whose style matches our vision, we'll send plenty of work their way. The best way to impress us would be to send us a sample or three based on some of the stories we've already published either in the magazine or the website, and we can take it from there.

We've an anniversary to celebrate. We've always thought that science fiction and fantasy have enduring charm and far-reaching influence, but this year's anniversary is a delightful reminder of just how long we've been able to read quality genre fiction. One hundred years ago, in 1923, *Weird Tales* began publishing its iconic mix of fantasy, horror and the supernatural. H.P Lovecraft, Robert E Howard, Robert Heinlein, Robert Bloch and Ray Bradbury were among the many writers who appeared in Weird Tales, often at the start of their careers, so it's probably no exaggeration to suggest that without _Weird Tales_, fantasy and horror writing as we know it today probably would look very different. It ran until 1954, an age in publishing – and has been described as 'the most influential of all fantasy magazines' (Robert Weinberg). Weird indeed that it should be 100 years old. Many followed – _Amazing, Astounding, Galaxy, Asimov's_ and the rest – but _Weird Tales_ predated most and has left a lasting impression. Conan the Barbarian meets Cthulhu. Need I say more?

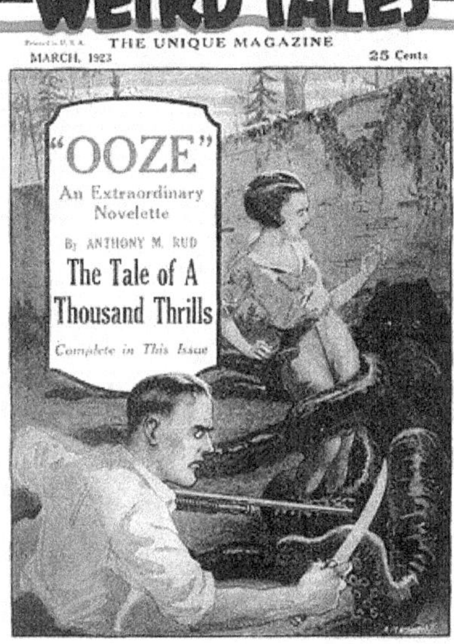

With the nine short stories we have in these pages we're carrying on a fine tradition for thoughtful, challenging stories popularised by the many fine magazines of the last hundred years. We kick off with Liam Hogan's _Vanishing Village,_ a story which wouldn't have looked out of place in _Weird Tales_ itself. The moral of the story? Beware locals offering gifts of food and drink in a crowded pub at the middle of a mysterious semi-abandoned village in the middle of nowhere. Also beware selkies bent on revenge – and see how Elisabeth Kauffman tackles that sea-sodden subject in _Foundering Fate._ Next up we have Egyptian writer Amal El Sayed with thoughtful and hard-hitting fantasy tale of ancient conflict: _Unmask Me_ won't be a story you'll quickly forget. We get lighter then - Steve Burford's _Knock Knock_ takes us in to the mind of a newly sentient AI with a sense of humour. Tee Linden's _Metamorphosis_ takes us back into darker territory – a fantasy tale of forest whisperings and discovery. Speaking of forests, we also have Dawn Vogel's _Family Tree_ and Elana Gomel's _Forests of Day and Night_ so there's definitely a theme emerging – both thoughtful fantasies from regular Wyldblood contributors. _Suspended Sentence_ by Maureen Bowden is all about trying to escape your fate, and, lastly _Gardens, Ghosts and War_ by H.L. Fullerton continues the nature theme, but this time there's a mysterious sword and a kid who can see dead people. No, not that story. Definitely no Bruce Willis.

Add in a couple of drabbles and the reviews and that's it for this issue. We hope you think these stories are as good as we do – if you love them, yet us know, let the authors know and tell your friends to give our little magazine a try – www.wyldblood.com

Enjoy the stories.

The Vanishing Village
Liam Hogan

Thomas stood on the dirt track and peered in both directions. An anxious ass, unable to work out which of two seemingly identical options was best. Left or right, there was nothing much to see, just more of the same, bleak, never-ending moorland, bisected neatly by this, for want of a better word, *road*, which thinned and vanished at each equally desolate horizon.

He had, and he still wasn't exactly sure how he'd managed it, got lost on the moors. Spent an exposed and miserable night out on it, the cold and damp working their way deep into his bones. This track was the first evidence he'd seen in--what? over sixteen hours?--that any humans other than himself had *ever* existed.

He'd check his phone for a more accurate time-keeping record and his hand did keep straying towards the pocket it was in, but there was no point in undoing the flap because it was flat, utterly drained by his in-vain search for reception, for a signal that would tell him where the hell he was. He'd packed a back-up compass--all very boy scout, you can never be too prepared--but perhaps he should have checked it before he'd left the safety of London, because the thing was playing silly buggers, never staying true. Under yesterday's monotonously grey skies he might have spent the increasingly fraught hours before dusk going round in circles, and he only knew he wasn't still doing so on this just as grey morning, because this was the first time he'd come across anything half as promising as a *road*.

None of which helped him decide which way to walk it. All other points of the malfunctioning compass were out of the equation, leaving him with this seemingly simple, binary choice.

He'd been exhilarated when he'd stumbled across the path, even one that wasn't much more than muddy patches slicing through the heather and hummocks of grass. Hummocks he'd been wearily stepping-stone across, already caught out one time too many by the foul smelling puddles of brackish water that lurked between and beneath. A straight line, of regular-ish width, meant that something must use it and it must lead somewhere. But towards civilisation, or away from it?

It was an important distinction. He only had his day-pack with him, a waterproof and a single change of clothes. His water bottle was empty and rattling, and his collection of energy bars was a handful of wrappers and the distant and rumbling memory.

It must, he decided, be the exhaustion that was fogging his brain, making him hesitate. The exhaustion, the cold, the hunger, perhaps even dehydration. How long had he already been stood here? Again, his hand strayed towards his useless phone, but he forced it to change direction. He'd let the fates decide. He extracted his useless compass and held it flat on his palm. The needle wavered and then settled, pointing roughly down the path that stretched to his left.

So be it. Even if it only led to a shepherd's shack, or some long abandoned mine, it had to be better than standing here, waiting for a bolt from the blue to show him the way. Or better yet a search party, come looking when he failed to arrive at the B&B he'd booked for last night.

Though, he mused, pocketing his compass again and adjusting the straps on his bag, no-one actually *knew* he was hiking across the moors to get there. No-one knew he'd deliberately got off one train stop early, and had intended to walk one stop beyond the B&B and indulge in a leisurely pub lunch before jumping back on the train to complete his journey. Only if he didn't turn up at his parents' in Whitby this evening might someone raise the alarm, and that would surely mean another night out on the moors. Thomas shuddered at the thought.

Trudging along once more, his legs tight and stiff from even a few minutes of stillness, it was easy to see why his grandma had been so full of warnings and stories of these forlorn, nameless places. Getting lost was always the start of one of those tales, which often seemed to involve rather cruel and easily offended pixies or fairies. Though the only one that had really scared him--and if he wasn't so tired he would have chuckled at the memory--were the redcaps, a band of murderous goblins whose distinctive headgear was dyed by gruesome means, and who were always on the search for fresh 'paint'. But even they had quickly lost their power because Thomas always baulked at the very first part of Grandma's stories, the getting lost bit. Even as a kid it had seemed ridiculous to contemplate being lost anywhere in the UK, with the possible exception of somewhere deep in Scotland. The North York Moors weren't the dark, ancient forests of the Brother's Grimm, in which straying from the path was so unwise. Here, surely, there would always be a road, or a set of electricity pylons marching into the distance, or a drawn-out line of other cagouled hikers following National Trust acorns. Or houses with smoke drifting from chimneys, or the distant spire of a church...

Or heck, just airplanes in the sky. That alone would be a welcome sign of humanity, a clue that just beyond the horizon all the stuff he was so used to was still there, waiting. He might even be able to use them as a rough navigational guide. He was so used to seeing planes constantly above him in London, to unconsciously tracking their regular flight paths, that their absence was almost alarming. Thomas wasn't sure if the cloud cover was simply too low, or if there were no flight paths that crossed the moors. The former, most likely. Though he guessed there weren't any airports nearby, so it wasn't surprising if any contrails were well above the ever prevalent clouds, high enough that no sound penetrated the desultory rustle of the rushes, or the steady drip of some brackish pool, or the heavy squelch of his not as waterproof as he had hoped hiking boots. Where would the nearest airport be? Newcastle? That wouldn't be anything as busy as even the smallest of London's four. One flight every half an hour, perhaps?

These and other mostly circular thoughts kept his mind busy as he schlepped onwards, over a dreary landscape which finally began to show signs of change, the path gently sloping. He was relieved to see the way led downwards and not just because of the ache in his legs. Downwards meant rivers, and hopefully, busier roads, and a town, and--

And yes! The track curved, cutting back on itself as the slope steepened. From its apex there opened up a valley some way below him, with a cluster of trees and a silver thread winding through it and--hallelujah!--a rooftop of grey slate, mottled with lichen. And another.

He almost broke into a run at the sight, at the thought of imminent rescue. But the path, switching back and forth to manage the gradient, still had a way to go and his legs didn't. *Patience*. It wouldn't be long now. There would be a little village shop down there, a combined post-office and everything else, a rack of dated, colour-bleached touristy postcards for hikers passing through to send back home. And a pub! There would be a pub with food and drink. A chance to recharge his phone, or to make use of (did such things still exist?) a payphone, to order a taxi and damn the cost.

Only, as he got closer, as the trees that shrouded the view opened up again to give him a new perspective, his spirits sank and he chewed at his chapped lips. No signs of wood smoke from the rooftops. No telegraph poles, or satellite dishes, or even rusty, defunct TV aerials. And no cars, or for that matter, *people*.

The village, as far as he could tell, lay abandoned. The windows, windowless; the doors, door-less. Gaping holes of black...

He felt a real pang of fear. He'd invested so much into getting here. *Everything*, he told himself, though he'd read enough tales of survival in extremis to suspect that wasn't strictly true. But what if this was a dead-end, civilisation lying at the *other* end of the dratted road?

Perhaps there might still be a stand-pipe or, in the worst case scenario he'd have to brave the water from the river and hope that this spot was isolated enough that it wasn't contaminated. And then he'd follow the river wherever it went next. The thought of climbing back up the hill and crossing the moor back the way he had come was... unthinkable.

The river was loud now and, as he completed what he felt sure must be the last switchback, he could glimpse the surprisingly hunched shape of a stone bridge that spanned it, leading into the ghost town. Only, as the road straightened and passed through an arch of overhanging trees, their mossy trunks guarded by thick clusters of funghi that he might have been tempted by if he had anyway to tell what was poisonous, and what was not, he could have laughed and called himself an idiot. The doom, such that it was, had all been in his mind. It wasn't a ghost town at all. No cars, sure, and no telephone wires, but this village was definitely populated, the houses were occupied, their gardens neat and tidy. Somewhere he could hear the sound of someone chopping wood. It was almost like he was coming down into a different village from the one he'd seen from above. There was the distinctive smell of a peat fire and glancing upwards he saw a chimney, extruding faint wisps of the fragrant smoke. It must be harder to spot, when he was above it. There might be freshly baked bread from such a fire. Or soup. He was almost salivating.

The crest of the tall bridge blocked his view and for a horrid moment, as he stumbled up the ancient stones, he half-wondered which village he would see when he came back down the other side.

The empty one, lifeless, deserted, or the one with flowers in windowsill planters and the sound of people and of chickens?

Thank god it was the latter. He staggered towards it, knees protesting, and found himself swaying outside the first of the stone and slate houses, wondering if he had the energy to open the little white gate and navigate the gravel path up to the front door.

He didn't need to. A movement in a vegetable patch to one side became a women, straightening up to her full height and regarding him with something akin to bemused curiosity.

"Ma'am?" Thomas croaked. "Could I trouble you for a glass of water?"

"From the looks, you need a whole lot more than *that*." She smiled and Thomas was struck by how insanely beautiful she was, much more so than he might have first thought. "Come in, come in! Before you *fall* in. Got lost out on the moors, did you?"

Sheepishly, tongue-tied, he nodded, staggering his way across the threshold, his leg clattering against the gate post, the clunk of his pocketed phone suggesting it might have come off even worse.

"The name's Magrite." The way she said it, it made him think of *may regret*. "And yours?"

"Thomas," he said and there was an echo of the stammer he hadn't had since he was knee-high to a grasshopper, since he'd been a wide-eyed kid listening to his grandma's scary tales.

"Well *Thomas*. Welcome to our little village. We don't, as it happens, get many visitors. But you're most welcome nonetheless."

Entering the cool dark of the cottage Thomas almost tripped over the stone lintel, a firm arm was all that kept him upright.

"Oh, you poor lamb..." He was guided to a sturdy wooden chair. "Let me get you that water." There were sounds around him over the ringing in his ears. A cupboard being opened, the rattle and clink of a pottery lid being removed and then--

"*Drat*. I'm sorry, Thomas. It's thirsty work, tending my garden! But never fear, I'll pop out to the well. Won't be a moment."

The cottage brightened as the door was re-opened, and then darkened again. In her absence Thomas took in his surroundings. Something he hadn't been able to do, before, the gloom revealing its secrets only slowly and no match for Magrite's beauty. The inside of the cottage was homely but spartan. And *very* old fashioned. No signs of electricity, no fridge, or microwave, or even lights, candles and lanterns not counting. Not even a proper sink, though there was a stone trough perched high on a wooden stand. The bowls stacked up next to it were also mostly wood, a few of rough pottery. A couple of small copper pots and pans hung above, the colour as red as Magrite's hair. In one corner stood a strange thing like a low three-legged stool, but with a pole that would prevent anyone sitting on it, something he'd seen on Bargain Hunt: a medieval implement for washing sheets, apparently. This was a village that time, or at least progress, had forgotten. There was nowhere in this house to charge his phone. He extracted it from his pocket, remembering the clunk it had received. A spidery crack spread across the lower half of the screen. He'd have cursed, but maybe in the grand scheme of things this was kind of trivial.

The cup that Magrite filled from her pitcher was also wooden, which he might have turned his nose up at if he'd been offered a choice and if he wasn't so parched. But the water it contained was cold and delicious. Maybe it was just his dire need, but he could barely restrain himself as he gulped it down. "More," he gasped, water dripping down his chin.

Magrite frowned and gently took the empty cup from him, fingers brushing his. "Not so fast, Thomas. Take it easy. Why don't you tell me your story?"

And so he did, interspersed by refilled cups of sweet, pure, cold water, until he didn't feel the need to gulp it down, until he could relinquish his grip, the cup not fully drained. He told her everything, aware that as he did his accent was trying to revert to something half forgotten, an attempt to match the lilt in her voice, the musical way some words expanded to include an extra syllable. It wasn't entirely successful, sounding forced and fake and still remaining resolutely southern, an anaemic, de-regionalised London accent, with only the odd word betraying his early years as a northerner.

Magrite didn't share much about herself in return. But that didn't matter, because she promised him food and, though they had no phone--no telephones at all, mobile or otherwise!-- in a little while, they'd go down to the pub and see if anyone was willing to take him on to the next town downstream. Though it was *quite* the way and it would be best if he was fully recovered first--a message? To his parents? Who were expecting him?--She'd see what she could do, but anyway she had a spare room and wouldn't it be much better if he rested here overnight?

He was surprised, when she lit the lanterns, how much light they spilled, how dark the cottage had become. How gloomy the view from the small windows. Dusk! His stomach rumbled, reminding him that it must almost be a full day since he'd last eaten anything at all. Another rumble, accompanied by a sloshing gurgle from all the water he had drunk.

Magrite ruefully shook her head. "Will you look at me, I promised you sustenance and terrible host that I am, I've kept you talking for hours! But the inn will be open, now, Thomas. Good, hearty food. And I dare say you'll be ravenous enough for the both of us."

Thomas protested that she'd been more than kind, feeling the flush on his cheeks as he did, though she shook her head again, as if to acknowledge he was merely being gallant and she had, in some fashion, utterly failed in her duties as host. But wasn't that his fault? He could have told her no more than why he'd been up on the moors and where he needed to get to. All the rest, his life story, complete with self-deprecating account of former girlfriends who were no long his, and workmates for whom he didn't exist, outside of the hours of nine to five...

She reached out and took his hand. The feeling was electric. And all one way; her grip firm and dry and somehow perfect, whereas his was embarrassingly weak and uncertain, damp with perspiration and god knows what else from his time on the moor, the crescent moons of his nails black with filth. He felt the need to apologise, to scrub himself clean from head to toe. To shave, to go for the most expensive manicure he could imagine, and then to undergo a vigorous six month training regime that would somehow give him complete mastery over the exact pressure to exert, and yet make it casually obvious the degree of restraint that he was exhibiting, all before trying again and perhaps then, and only then, being on level par with this bewitching woman. But there was no time for any of that, as Magrite pulled him to his reluctant feet.

"Come on, I can already hear the music!"

So could he, though he was surprised at that; how long had it been playing for? Quick, energetic notes that got stronger on the short walk through town, past tightly packed cottages almost identical to Magrite's, each well tended and many with the soft glow of lanterns or candles in the windows or through open doorways.

The pub didn't bother with a sign and didn't need one, the largest, brightest, and noisiest of the village's buildings (no church or chapel to compete with, which might have puzzled Thomas if he'd bothered to think on it).

The sounds of some frenetic jig peppered the air, and, though from outside it looked like there was no room for any more, with already a handful of villagers hovering outside the stout wooden door and the open windows, Magrite somehow pushed through and, dragging Thomas with her, even managed to secure a table and two chairs, for which his blistered and sore feet were extraordinarily grateful.

Like his arrival at Magrite's cottage, it took a while for him to take it all in, especially as Magrite hadn't yet let go of his hand and all his attention seemed to be in his fingertips. But one thing was impossible to ignore; the way both the music and the hubbub of voices fell eerily silent, seemingly in time with their arrival. It was like one of those extremely local pubs in films, when a stranger walks in. Though perhaps, Thomas briefly thought, it was because it was Magrite that had walked in. She wasn't, he quickly found, the only female in there, even if they were in a distinct minority and Magrite was by far the most beautiful. So, no; it must be the stranger: *him*.

"Caught yourself another stray, Magrite?" a wry comment came at them, and Thomas looked up and up again into the rather dauntingly bewhiskered face of a brick-house of a man, who would have to stoop to avoid the pub's low beams, though if he did semi-regularly brain himself it might explain the darting, hostile look he was giving Thomas.

"Donegal, this here's Thomas," Magrite said. "Do be nice to him. Poor lamb has had a bit of an ordeal."

"Lamb?" he heard someone else mutter and looked in vain through the waists and arms and torsos for who it might be. "Fresh meat, anyways. Though why is it always Magrite who bags 'em?"

"She has her ways, does Magrite," came yet another voice, more reflective. "It's her *glamour*."

Envy, thought Thomas, was such an ugly thing. And not, he was fully aware, something that *he* usually provoked. But then, maybe that wasn't so weird, even if he hadn't been Magrite's guest. It was probably obvious to everyone he wasn't from around these parts, and might be equally obvious he was from London. Which must seem like some strange, exotic nirvana, compared to a village that didn't even connect to the grid. *Any* grid.

It was like something out of a 1970's horror film. Wicker Man, or some rural dystopia penned by John Wyndham. A close-knit community, somehow managing to keep itself apart, into which our plucky hero stumbles, the dark truths slowly being revealed along with an utterly contrived mechanism to make sure he couldn't escape... Though normally the outsiders would arrive as a couple, a blond, virginal girl to raise the stakes and to inflate the sense of foreboding peril.

Thomas glanced at Magrite and found her wryly watching him. Red haired, not blond and, though stunning, definitely *not* virginal. No innocent, she. There was something knowing, and vaguely carnal in her regard, that sent his gaze scurrying away, afraid of what dark truths he might discover in her eyes.

Two old fashioned tankards arrived, seemingly unbidden. Pewter, perhaps, from the dull shine and sound they made as Thomas and Magrite clinked them together. He'd have been happier with a standard pint glass, happier still with a choice. Thomas wasn't one for lagers, the gas sat heavy on his stomach and while some of his workmates could seemingly neck them as if drinking for England, even a single pint was likely to leave him feeling bloated.

But *this* beer... this beer was the best ale he'd ever tasted, hands down. Golden in colour, the aroma bright and enticing before his first sip. And that sip... impossibly it was even better than the exquisitely cool, refreshing water from Magrite's well. Almost floral, with the hops perfectly balancing the sweetness. It was ambrosia, nectar from the gods, heaven in a glass. Or a tankard. And maybe some of that was because of his lingering thirst, his hunger, and his relief at finding succour. Or the company, Magrite's eyes smiling over the rim of her tankard as she drank to match him. Or maybe it was something in the local water, the same earthy tang from Magrite's well, assuming the stuff was brewed on site.

And then--choirs of angels rejoice!--a meat pie appeared on an earthenware plate, swimming in thick brown gravy and surrounded by sliced green beans which, miracle upon miracles, hadn't been cooked down to a limp mush, which retained a pleasing fresh bite to them and, because genie's wishes came in threes, a bowl of skin-on chips, hot and salty and with perfect floury innards, and another of those pints to make it four. For a good few minutes, until his plate was licked clean, Thomas's attention was laser focused, sucking up the meaty, gamy aroma as he devoured the meal. When he neatly lined up his silver knife and fork it was almost with sorrow, because he was

fairly sure that given the chance he'd be able to polish off the same again, or at least to relish the challenge.

He felt like a king, now. As he leant back, grinning expansively, music started up as if on cue, and when he sought out the musicians--correctly assuming that there would be no jukebox, even of the ancient, select a record variety--he almost sprayed his latest mouthful of beer across the little table. By the huge hearth, three men sat on stools, hunched over their instruments, one on a fiddle, one on a flat drum that he held in the air--a bodhran?--and one on a tiny flute, almost a whistle. But it was the red caps they wore above wizened faces that deadened the grin that had been plastered on his face.

The drummer saw his gaping regard and grinned back with tombstone teeth. All three of them did, dipping their heads at him without missing a beat.

Thomas shivered, and then was distracted once more as a stool was slung towards their table. Even before it had stopped its rattle, the big guy-- Donegal, was sat there, looking like an overgrown and rather ill-tempered schoolboy.

The man pointedly ignored Thomas, rounding instead on Magrite, their conversation running too fast, or perhaps in some local dialect, for him to properly follow. But it was clear Donegal was upset and equally clear Magrite was standing her ground. It was also clear that the topic of their disagreement was him, Thomas.

It was painfully awkward. He didn't know the history between the two, and he hadn't--had he?--done anything to be the cause of such enmity. But Magrite *had* favoured him, had even offered him a bed for the night. Innocent though that offer might be, imagination would colour it a different hue, for those looking for offence. Well, it was none of his concern, as long as Donegal didn't do anything stupid.

Though maybe a peace offering would help?

"I'll get in another round, shall I?" Thomas said, not waiting for an answer before threading his way towards the back of the room, where the crowd was even thicker. They let him pass, where they could, and he backtracked where they couldn't, and all the while he was aware of being watched, and that this village really hadn't done itself any favours being so remote and cloistered, given the effects of a reduced gene pool, even if it did throw up the odd beauty like Magrite.

Finally, he broached at the bar. A single pull with no name or badge, a shelf half full of tankards, and little or nothing else, except the barman patiently waiting for his order.

"Three pints, please," he said, and then wondered if he should have returned the empties.

The barman nodded, and began pulling, and the delicious beery, hoppy aroma cut through the air. His wallet was waved away even in the act of reaching for it. "Your money's no good here," he was told, though of course his wallet didn't *have* any money, just a credit card and he couldn't see a reader anyway, not even one of those mobile ones, so he was delighted for the generosity. He collected the three tankards, concentrated on carrying them without spilling, and headed through the labyrinth of bodies back to his table.

Donegal looked up sourly at his return, not mollified even by the tankard Thomas lowered before him. It looked like the discussion had continued during his absence and it hadn't gone the big man's way.

"You ought to share, Magrite," Donegal said, a mixture of gruff and peevish. "*Rude* to be so selfish."

Thomas felt like telling him to get lost. That, at least for tonight, Magrite was his, or he was Magrite's, even if the full extent of the relationship was nothing more than a spare bed in a spare room. But the man was a bear and Thomas was drinking for free, and someone in here, *anyone*, even Donegal, might be the person who would give him a lift to the train station, or even, if he was polite and on his best behaviour, all the way to his parent's doorstep.

Magrite shrugged it off anyway, a deliberately casual sip of the beer as if laying ownership to it. And then she stood, and with a small bow, announced louder than was strictly necessary. "Well then, Donegal, I *shall* share."

She left a lengthy pause as a ripple of attentive silence radiated outwards. "A *tale*, that is."

The inn chuckled in delight.

"But which story should I tell?" she asked, inviting a slew of requests; the White Mare, or Wade and Bell, or "something with bogarts!"

"Only one tale to be told, Magrite," Donegal said, into a gap between the other suggestions, something sly and hard in his voice. "Tell our visitor the tale of the vanishing village."

There was laughter at that, though Thomas wasn't sure why, since it was obvious Donegal was being a jerk. He cradled his ale in his hands and smiled inanely back at them, as Magrite slowly nodded her head and took to the cleared space near the fire, lit by ruddy flames that made her hair glow like molten lava.

An expectant hush descended even as Magrite somehow became more animated, her posture reminding Thomas of a cat ready to pounce, her emerald gaze slowly scanning the many faces in the crowd, lingering for a long moment on his.

A wry quirk of her lips gave her smile an uneven aspect, sardonic, playful, a sign that what she was about to relate might not be entirely truthful. And then she began:

"There was once a village in these parts, not so very unlike ours."

More laughter, at that. An in-joke then, this. A tale told to the incredulous. A tale told, and retold, throughout the cold winter months, with no television or pub quizzes to distract the audience.

"It began as a slate-mining village," she went on, "and then, beneath the slate, they discovered tin, their excavations carving ever deeper into what was already a narrow gorge, houses built wherever the miners exhausted the deposits. Tin that made the pewter tankards from which we all gratefully drink."

A forest of arms shot into the air, each proudly holding its tankard, some of contents spilled in good humoured mirth. Thomas belatedly and only half heartedly joined in, and as he did he could tell this tale must be a favourite, told often enough that the audience knew all the beats, the points at which to respond.

Oral storytelling, he thought, marvelling that this tradition was what once passed for entertainment, and feeling an odd loss that the rest of the country, the civilised world, with its amplified sound systems and projector TVs showing sports or music videos or whatever, was missing out on such simple pleasures. Especially when told by a beauty like Magrite.

"But there were others who considered the gorge *their* sacred home. Others who had been there long before there was tin, or slate. Others who weren't happy with the noisy village, and the noisy, uncouth villagers, with their dogs and their iron--"

There was a loud hiss from all around at that, which surprised Thomas. Though, come to think of it, what with pewter and wood and stone and with the lack of cars, had he seen any proper metal at all?

"--and their workings, bespoiling the river and the earth, belching filth and flames into the air. And these people, these ancient ones, they were determined to take back and restore what was rightfully theirs.

"Now, likely as not, and if not you haven't been listening, you've all heard tales of travellers blundering into a fey feast, crossing the bounds between our world and theirs and what misfortune befalls them, especially if they are unwise. If they fail to give the proper respect to the little people. Well, here, with the fae on the warpath, the situation was somewhat reversed.

"Because the fey decided that the only way to get back what had been stolen, and to protect what was left, was to shift the *whole* village across to the other side, to make off with it, if you will."

She paused again, scanning the audience, the silence seemingly a beat too long as if she had forgotten the thread, but she was too much the master storyteller for that.

"Almost the whole village," she declared into the hush. "The church, alas, didn't make it."

More laughter at that. More nodding of heads and puffs of smoke--smoke! People were actually smoking, indoors. And not vape sticks, or e-cigarettes or even real cigarettes, these were pipes, some thin, and of pale pottery, some fat, wide bowls of soot-dark wood, all filling the air with a purple haze and a sweet, caramel smell of distant memory.

"The fey held a gathering for the feast of Mabon. And they decided to hold it not in one of their small copses or within the safety of a fairy ring or the standing stones on the crest of a windswept hill, but on the tin-mining village's small, neat, village green. A grand picnic they set out, with food and drink and music galore."

A clash of notes from fiddles and bodhran and flutes met this, the musicians laughing as they lowered their instruments again and retook their tankards.

"Now the villagers, each assuming that their neighbour had put on the unexpected feast, and their neighbours assuming *they* had, a celebration of the village's wealth and growth, and no-one wanting to ask in case it turned out they weren't, after all, invited; well, the villagers were all more than happy to crash this gathering of the fey. And every single one in the village, every man, woman and child, even the wee bairns, joined in the picnic, not waiting for any announcements or hosts to appear, tucking into all that fairy food laid out so enticingly on the village green."

Thomas listened as the story played out the way it had to, half his attention on the use of techniques he'd learnt in a creative writing course after University, when, despite his newly minted job, he was still unsure what he should be doing with his life. *This* story had it all. The conflict, steadily building. The rule of three. Elements from the hero's journey, leading to a point of no return. Fate, sealed. It was very much a classical story in its shape, though not one he'd ever heard tell before. As Magrite had said, it was unusual for a whole village to fall under a fairy spell, odder still for that spell to change the nature of the fae themselves, binding them as well as the villagers together in one place, making it so that you couldn't tell them apart.

And when it came to an end, the audience hanging on Magrite's slowly softening words until the dreadful final coda, the ultimate payback for rules unwittingly transgressed, the sneering moment of disrespect and disbelief, and the denouement; the refreshing and maintaining of the spell of concealment, of protection, by attracting a new victim to be sacrificed every seven years, (a neat way to make what was a historical story seem more current), Thomas had no hesitation in joining in with the thunderous applause, the stomping of feet that kept hands free for their drinks, the wooden floorboards bouncing under the assault. Magrite gave a delightful bow and her place was retaken by the musicians--a different set of three, no redcaps, these--who quickly tuned their instruments but then fell into a quiet lull, as if waiting for their allotted timeslot to begin, not that Thomas could see a clock anywhere.

"How did you like my story, Thomas?" Magrite asked, returning to the table, the inn implausibly even busier now, their chairs squeezed together until they sitting so close he could feel the heat from her leg, and wondered if she felt his.

Thomas shook his head, feeling a little woozy, a vague sense of the unreal that comes with being pleasantly drunk, though surely he hadn't had enough beer for that, not yet? He hesitated and almost found himself saying the right thing, the *polite* thing. But enchanting though the story had been, it was one of those impossible tales. And really, he didn't *want* to point out its obvious and grievous flaw, to spoil it for Magrite, for her attentive audience, who despite the hubbub seemed to be leaning in, waiting for his answer, but how could he *not*? A story could be as fantastical as it liked, but it had to hang together, had to play by its own rules.

"If as you say," he pointed out, slowly, deliberately, "no-one from the village was ever seen again, then who is there to tell their tale?"

And the laughter was back and went on until Thomas felt like his face was aflame.

"A fair comment, Thomas," Magrite said, nodding and seemingly unoffended. "No one *could* tell that tale, except..." And the touch at his leg suddenly felt like a vice.

"Except?" Thomas belatedly, realised that his question was also part of the tale. That he, the stranger, had been set up. That was why they were all still listening, waiting for her replies, and his reaction, for the end of this story. Was he truly so predictable?

Probably.

"Except, those within that village itself, Thomas. And the generations that came after, who kept the story alive." She did that pause thing again, waiting until you almost thought there was no more to say. "And, of course, to anyone who accidentally wanders in, once every seven years, and has the misfortune to fall prey to the same enchantments, the same spell."

All eyes were on Thomas. Somehow, he was not only part of the telling, but part of the tale itself. The village in the story was the one he was in, right now.

Ridiculous! Nothing but the punchline to a camp-fire tale, the shiver of fear when the barrier between make-believe and reality seemed for a moment to waver.

So why did his stomach lurch as though he'd just plunged into an abyss? Why was he driven to defend himself? "I haven't crossed into fairyland!" he protested, wide-eyed, though there was that arch of trees he'd passed through, dotted with toadstools, or the steep-sided, oddly arched bridge... "I haven't feasted! I haven't eaten fairy food, or drank fairy drink..."

He trailed off, at the memory of the water from well, at the meaty pie, the chips, and at the divine, strong ale. He came to a complete stop, at the look from Magrite. The cool, appraising gaze morphed into a smile, but a different smile from before. A smile that wasn't to be shared. At least, not with Thomas.

"Well, Thomas," she said, lifting her tankard in a mocking salute. "I guess you have now."

Liam Hogan is an award-winning short story writer, with stories in Best of British Science Fiction and in Best of British Fantasy (NewCon Press). He's been published by Analog, Daily Science Fiction, and Flame Tree Press, among others. He helps host live literary event Liars' League, volunteers at the creative writing charity Ministry of Stories, and lives and avoids work in London. More details at http://happyendingnotguaranteed.blogspot.co.uk

Foundering Fate
Elisabeth Kauffman

Trigger warnings: domestic partner violence

"That's weird," Angelo said, stepping forward and leaning over the splintery rail and gaping at the flotilla of sea lions below. "They never stop barking."

Luna's stomach dropped. She should never have agreed to this date at Pier 39 in the first place. Since things had ended with Cliff, she'd pretty much exclusively dated women anyhow. All two times in the past two years. She'd only swiped right on Angelo to prove two points to Eve. One, she wasn't afraid of men or sex; and two, all men were narcissists and/or completely unreliable.

Case in point. "Come on, let's go." She pulled on the sleeve of Angelo's T-shirt as he leaned further over the railing toward the water. "I want a churro." She held herself back from the sightline of so many California sea lions basking on the floating docks. The uncomfortable silence, punctuated by the lapping wake of a passing ferry, and the whisper of leathery sea lion bodies shifting across one another, left no cover for her.

"No look, they're all turning this direction!" Angelo laughed and pointed like he was eight. "So weeeird!" He leaned back over, ignoring Luna's protests.

"Look, I don't like sea lions, ok? I just want to…"

The air felt stagnant suddenly. Their whiskery brown faces all turned in her direction. Luna's vision blurred and she felt her knees wobble. It was too much. The weighted stare of all those dark eyes, the dead fish smell, the body odor of a hundred writhing pinnipeds piled on one another in the hot October sun. She had to leave. Now.

"Fine. I'm out of here." She power-walked away from the tourist attraction, which was luckily nowhere near as crowded as historically, before the pandemic year, when people had been unafraid to gather. The hollow husk of the pier should have made her melancholy, and if she'd stop to consider it, maybe it would now. But her only concern was getting as far away from here as possible.

Her date caught up to her a few seconds after she hit the pier's front entrance.

"What's your deal?" he huffed, his face flushed with effort and entitlement.

"I told you, I don't like the sea lions." Or rather, they didn't like her… not anymore… She'd been one of them once. But that was before she'd lost her skin. Or rather, before it had been taken from her.

"Huh?"

"Well, this was nice…" she held out her hand, hoping to make her escape official.

"Aw, no, come on. Don't say goodbye yet." Angelo crossed his arms and stepped back. "Didn't you just say you want a churro?" He jerked his head toward the food cart 20 feet back down the pier, toward the shops, and the carousel. He flashed her a winning smile, his mouth full of straight, white teeth. "At least let me buy you a churro."

Late that night, after predictably disappointing sex at Angelo's place in the Outer Sunset, Luna found herself alone, standing on the cold sand of Ocean Beach, the waning moon climbing above her. The Pacific Ocean in all its inky vastness stretched out before her. She felt the pull of the salt water in her belly, and her bones ached with the power of each wave crashing onto the shore. Her skin itched with the desire to dive into the waves. To feel the ice-cold embrace of home enfold her again. To wash the humanity off of her. But the closer she got to the water line, the harder her heart pounded, stealing her breath. She couldn't do it. She had never wanted anything more and yet felt so powerless to achieve it.

She stood with her arms wrapped around her, toes just out of reach of the salty waves, tears streaming down her face flushed with the chill wind of the San Francisco Bay. The call of a seal out on the water somewhere, shrouded by fog, sent a shiver down her spine.

She crouched and lifted a sand dollar off the wet sand, felt its myriad feet tickling her palm as it searched for familiar ground, disoriented and out of its element. If she left it where she'd found it, with the swiftly receding tide, a sea gull would gut it at dawn. She flipped it over and examined the feet wriggling and writhing for a few moments before skipping it like a stone off the next incoming wave. It bounced four times and sank with a satisfying *plop* a safe distance beyond the break and the low-tide edge. Rescued.

If only someone could do that for her.

"You know what you have to do if you want to go back." Eve's dusky voice made Luna flinch and sink lower toward her coffee mug and the cracked Formica surface of a corner table at the stubbornly open and empty 24-hour diner. Lock-down restrictions had eased, but people's fears had not.

"Yeah," Luna grumbled, staring into the black liquid as if coffee scrying would reveal the answer she needed. "It's not *what* I need to do. It's *how*."

"What do you mean how?" Eve scoffed, her bottle-black asymmetrical bob curtaining her flawless, alabaster forehead. "It's simple enough. You just..." She made a wringing motion with her hands and stuck her tongue out in Luna's direction.

Luna sagged further down into the booth. That's what she got for asking a siren for advice. It was in Eve's nature to be ruthless, exacting. If only Luna could channel that somehow.

"It's not that easy, and you know it," she said, shooting Eve a resentful look. "I can't just take a life. I can't even squash a bug on purpose..." Even if she could do what it took to get a selkie skin, bonding it to herself would be tricky. The magic didn't always work the way it was supposed to. Probably because you weren't supposed to lose it in the first place.

Eve rolled her eyes. "It's not that hard either. If you want that part of your life back, you do what you have to."

"Could you? Do it? If you had to," she asked, scrutinizing her friend for a shred of the truth behind the facade. "Kill one and... you know..."

"If it meant the difference between being stuck here for the rest of my life or being free?" Eve met her gaze with ice blue eyes, held it for a moment, then shrugged. "Yeah, I could do it."

Her heart sank. Eve was right. That was the only way. And if she was right, then Luna was stuck here. A tear escaped from the corner of her eye and dripped down onto the table. Another followed. "I don't think I can. And I don't think I can live here like this

forever, either. It's been two years. It's not getting any easier."

Eve reached across the table and patted Luna's arm, her talon-like nails pricking Luna's soft tan skin. "Give it a hundred years. You'll change your mind."

Luna barked a husky laugh through her tears. "That's what you said about Tinder."

She had thought she was going to die that night, almost two years ago. Cliff had scared her with violent outbursts before, but never like that. The houseboat railing dug into her lumbar and her hair brushed the surface of the harbor as he pressed against her, pinning her with his weight, his meaty fist wrapped around her throat. Screaming obscenities. Accusing her of trying to run off. Furious that he'd caught her searching for her selkie skin again.

Their relationship had gone from bad to worse. What had started as a night of indiscretion a year earlier had spiraled into fear, gas lighting, manipulation. She had lost all sense of self. She could hardly remember what it was to be happy, to be free. Of course she'd been trying to leave.

"Please..." she choked. Tears streamed down her face, blurring her vision as she flailed and kicked and scratched at his face. Her eyes bulged; her lungs burned with lack of oxygen. She felt the edges of unconsciousness closing in. And then he... slipped. That was what she told the cops, anyhow. There was water on the deck, and he was blindingly drunk. He must have slipped, thank god, and let her go.

Next thing she knew she was gasping and choking on the boards, heaving huge sobs that didn't help her breathe any more than Cliff's fists had. And Cliff was gone, drowned and washed out to sea by the current.

But she had seen it. The sea lion that grabbed Cliff's ankle and dragged him off the boat. She couldn't tell the cops that. They'd never believe her. They barely believed her as it was. Domestic dispute gone wrong. That was how they were spinning it. The neighbors all claimed they had heard nothing. It was only after Cliff's job reported him missing two days later that anyone even bothered to check.

After the police had finished questioning her, then she finally dared to believe he was gone, and began searching for her skin again. He was dead, and that meant she was free. She should have felt it, felt her power revert back to her. She should have automatically known where the skin was. So why didn't she?

She tore the houseboat apart, dumping Cliff's musty, broken belongings into the harbor. The houseboat wasn't that big. Where could he have hidden it? She ripped open the kitchen cabinets with a crash of broken glass and crockery. Nothing. Her body shook, and bile burned the back of her throat. Something was wrong. She should be free. He was dead. He couldn't hurt her anymore. She sank into the lumpy couch, wrapped her arms around herself to try and calm the shivering, curled into a ball dripping with cold sweat. He was dead, so why couldn't she move on from this nightmare? She didn't get up, even after the sun set and the place went dark. She drifted in and out of sleep. How much time passed? Hours, days?

Eve came and went during that time, bringing food, alcohol, and reports from the outside world. Sometimes all she did was curl up next to Luna on the couch, press a hip against her, loop an arm around her motionless body. Luna barely registered her. She felt disconnected from her body, as though she floated above it. Easier not to feel for now.

And then one afternoon, while she was lying staring down on herself as her consciousness floated at the ceiling, she saw the box.

It was small. Mother-of-pearl. The size of her palm. Tucked onto the high shelf that ran around the whole boat, just below the ceiling. Too nice to belong in this run-down life.

She scrambled to reach it, knocking over the wooden chair on her way back to the couch. Licking the salt from her lips, she turned the box over in her hands, heart in her throat. It was too small to hold her seal skin, but something told her the answer lay within. Heart thudding, she hesitated, not sure she wanted to know it.

"What is that?" Eve asked, snatching the box away from her. "Is that his?"

Luna nodded, lump in her throat, eyes fixed on the silvery rainbow of the polished sides of the box.

Eve didn't bother asking for permission, popped the box open with a jerk of her wrist. A key to a safe deposit box landed with a thud, and scrap of paper, charred at the edges, fluttered into Luna's lap. She recognized his handwriting.

There's no escaping. No finding your skin and returning to the sea. The skin is gone. I burned it after the first time you tried to leave me. You're mine forever now.

She should have died. That would have been better than wasting away like this. Why couldn't he have just killed her? Useless piece of shit. Instead he stole and destroyed the most vital part of her essence. He didn't even invite her to the bonfire he made of her. She wasn't sure what was worse. That he had done it, or that he had let her believe she still had a chance to be free.

If she had known what he was like, maybe she wouldn't have been so careless. Maybe she would have guarded the skin more closely. But she hadn't known, hadn't fathomed that he would figure out a way to wreck her forever. When she'd met him, he had told her he loved her. And she'd believed him at first. She should never have trusted him.

"There has to be another way," she whined. "I can't continue on like this anymore." She fingered the safe deposit box key, tied on a strand of yarn she wore around her neck.

Eve rolled her eyes and groaned. "Are all you selkies this spineless?" She eyed Luna with feigned disdain, but Luna could see sympathy slip into her friend's gaze.

"I just wish the sea lions didn't … look at me the way they do … like I'm about to murder one of them."

"Well _we_ know you aren't," Eve said, "but they don't know that. And even if they could give you one, which they can't, they're not just going to give you a skin. They already took a big risk by stepping in and saving you that night."

"I know… but what if I found one that was … like… already dying?" Luna asked for what felt like the millionth time. Even as she asked it, she knew what the answer would be. She could never willingly take another life.

"You just need to get back on the dating scene. Maybe you'll meet someone and you won't want to leave so bad." Eve batted her eyelashes at the only other customer in the diner with them that night. The man, in his 50s, dribbled coffee down his shirt he was so discombobulated by her.

"Mmmmm…. That's your answer for everything, Eve. But I'm just not interested anymore." Angelo had called a couple of times after that first date. But she didn't have the energy to keep stringing him along.

A full moon rose glistening over the city skyline. Luna stood at the edge of the water at the end of the marina's jetty, listening to the soft crash of wave against rock, and the deep gulp from the ceramic and stone pipes of the wave organ, an interactive art piece installed in the '80s. Sounds from the deep. Voices that whispered secrets that she had no choice but to keep.

Another year gone. Another year with Cliff dead and her skin destroyed, stuck in this interminable in between. It had been almost a decade since that horrible night. Eve said not to count the years, that it would only make her more depressed, but Luna couldn't help herself. It was the only way she felt marked her existence, or made her real anymore.

She'd accepted fate… sort of… At

least she'd made peace with the sea lions. She promised never to harm one of them, and they had helped her begin to reconnect to her power again. She would never be able to return to the sea in her true form. But she could feel the vibrations of magic in the world again.

She bought a place in Sausalito with the insurance money after Cliff's houseboat burned down. She'd used the key and found the policy in that safe deposit box. It was the least he could do, even though she was sure he never intended for her to benefit from it.

She took up team swimming in the San Francisco Bay. The salt water sliding over her skin reminded her of all she'd lost, but she just pretended she didn't mind anymore. She was a good swimmer. And some days she felt like she'd almost made friends. Maybe this was all she needed.

A footstep crunched on the crushed shell path, and she turned, spotted the young person stumbling forward. Tears glistened off their face, reflecting moonlight on the water, bright enough to see the bruise on their cheek, bright enough to recognize the pain and the fear.

"They said you'd know how to help me," came the whisper. The hairs on Luna's arm rose.

"Who did?" She already knew the answer, but she had to ask.

"The sea lions…" their voice broke in a sob. "My skin… it's missing…" The shadowy form sank, and Luna slipped down next to them on the ground.

"Not gone, not destroyed, just taken?" she asked. They nodded, more tears splashing onto the dirt and crushed shells beneath them.

Her heart pounded, awake after so much time asleep. She might be stuck here for the rest of time, but this one didn't have to be. This was something she could use her magic for. To help discover what had been lost or stolen. This was what would make her life of exile worth living. She gripped the wrists of this kindred spirit.

"Don't worry, my love," she whispered, fierce and strong. "We'll find it."

Elisabeth Kauffman is the Marketing Director for the San Francisco Writers Conference and an independent editor of fiction and memoir. She released a tarot deck for writers in January of 2021. This is her debut fiction publication.

Unmask Me
Amal El-Sayed

WAR IS COURAGE; WAR IS DUTY; WAR IS GLORY. These are the words that I have lived by since I was seven.

"War is courage, Naria. Limbs can be lost, but the courage in your heart remains," the General says. I am seven years old, and my father is missing a leg. "There is still a lot an amputee can do for the war." *An amputee!* He means my father; the word sounds foreign to my ears. My father's eyes are frenzied, searching the room for something that is not there. I wonder what he is searching for; I wonder if the war had severed more than his leg. His eyes refuse to land on the table where steel, metal, and lead are waiting to be fashioned into instruments of death. The General's eyes are filled with ire, his fervent gaze blaming my father for not holding on to his leg.

"War is duty, Naria. Your brother is old enough to join us now. It is his duty to serve this country," the General says. I am fourteen years old, and my baby brother is clutching a sword in his hands. He is holding it as if it were a toy, his innocent eyes alight with wonder. My father is holding his cane as if it were a lifeline, his eyes blazing with horror. The General's lower lip is twisted into a sneer; his eyes are hungry as he stares at my brother—another soldier to feed a never-sated beast.

"War is glory, Naria. Your mother died defending her home; she died a hero," the General says. I am sixteen years old, and my mother's eyes are frozen in a look of pure terror, her mouth open in a scream that never managed to escape her lips. My tears slide down her face as my fingers close

her eyes forever. The General's eyes are hungry, but this time his eyes are on me, not on my brother. There is a different hunger in them—a ravenous desire that makes me cross my arms over my chest and dig my fingers into my hands.

I am eighteen years old; I am a woman in a time of war. My hair is gathered under my kerchief; my fingernails are crusted with blood; my hands are littered with welts, and my back is bent with tragedy. I spend my days assembling weapons with my father: heaps of malleable metal and white-hot steel pressed together into deadly contraptions. A pang of gnawing guilt grows in my belly and slithers to my throat, suffocating me. I am manufacturing death in my tiny house, imperceptible blood covering my hands more and more each day. My world is on fire, and I am gathering more firewood.

The view from my window never changes: a labyrinth of grey structures and stone alleys interlocking together in an endless circle with the hulking figure of The Citadel looming above us all. We dwell on the outskirts of the kingdom, farther from the Citadel and closer to the Wall. The Wall is a monstrous edifice surrounding Keydonia's outskirts, obscuring the sun and delving half of the kingdom in shadows. Keydonia was once a place of sunlit archways, rainbow-coloured homes, and echoing laughter. It was more than just a land; it was a life worth fighting for. My ancestors took their very first cry as newborns on its ground, scraped their knees on its rocks, walked beside their first loves on its sidewalks, kissed under its trees, and danced under its moonlight. That is why when the war came, they fought for it ferociously, viciously, *mercilessly*. It is said that Lazom, Keydonia's neighbouring kingdom, used to be Keydonia's closest ally, but greed is a serpent that is never content with the offerings we give it. One of Lazom's kings coveted the riches of our mines, and Keydonia's king retaliated, setting his eyes on Lazom's sapphire-blue rivers and emerald-green fields. And so the war began and went on *and on and on.* No matter how much bloodshed it is fed, its hunger is never sated, its thirst is never quenched. It always demands *more, more, more.* And we, imperfect humans that we are, have no option but to oblige.

Long ago, the steppe between the two kingdoms used to be a map of interlocking trade roads. My mother used to tell me of firelit festivals on the steppe where Keydonians and Lazomians danced from sunset till sunrise. People lost themselves in a blur of dancing bodies and masked faces: beautiful creations of lace and leather that accentuated smiling eyes and rosy lips. Now, the steppe is a battlefield: a dance of blood-red death in a sea of black and golden masks. Every Keydonian wears the onyx-black mask of the wolves that roam our eastern forest, and every Lazomian dons the sun-golden mask of their first warlord. Masks used to unite; now they separate. For Keydonians, black equals friend; gold equals foe. But after each battle, only one colour prevails: the crimson red of shed blood.

The Keydonia of today is a kingdom built to withstand sieges and raise armies; it is not meant for dancing festivals and laughing children. There is no beauty here, only *safety*. Beauty, laughter, and sunshine are *'life'* things, and we cannot ask for life—only a little less death. But there is no safety in war, only the illusion of it. The illusion came apart on the day of *the incident*: the day every Kedydonian remembers and is desperate to forget. The incident is the only time the Wall has been breached. It is the same day our army left the kingdom for battle and left the women and children *safe* behind walls. Except it was not safe! The Dark Wraiths, the silent assassins of Lazom's army, slithered their way inside Keydonia and slaughtered a dozen of its women and children. They came cloaked in shadows and disappeared with no trace left behind except for the red rivers that soaked our streets. A message from Lazom's king: NO ONE IS SAFE! My mother was one of the incident's *casualties*. "A hero," the General called her, but in truth, she was a victim like all of us.

No woman is allowed to fight in Keydonia, but we have our own daily battles. I have tied a hundred tourniquets, sutured a thousand wounds, and told endless lies of *"You will make it"* as soldiers breathed their last breaths between my arms. I have been a weapons maker, a nurse, a cook, a washer, and sometimes a monk privy to a stranger's last words. I move amidst the steppe slowly today; the sun is scorching my face and the wind is biting my skin. I hear a groan nearby, and my eyes dart left and right till they land on a soldier with no armour. His leg is skewed at an odd angle — possibly broken, and there is a deep wound that runs across his lower waist, but I have seen enough to know that he has a good chance of surviving. I gently remove his wolf mask to reveal the face beneath it, only to be met by the most striking pair of eyes—as green as an enchanted forest, a rarity in Keydonia. *"Diabolus,"* they would say in Keydonia whenever a child is born with eyes the colour of the enemy's. Something in my soul stirs as I gaze into them. An *answering loss*—that is what I glimpse in his eyes, a loss that answers mine in ways I cannot comprehend. I bring the waterskin to his lips and force him to drink then deftly wrap a bandage around his wound. He grunts in pain, his calloused hand twitching. But instead of digging his hand into mine as so many others did before him, he grabs a rock and squeezes hard.

"I am Naria," I say. "Who are you?"

"Dead?" he asks/ answers.

My lips tug in a half smile. "No, alive." I interlock my fingers through his and squeeze. *"Alive,"* I repeat before his eyes drift shut and he is pulled into the land of nightmares.

"Over here," I shout as the infirmary cart is hauled by.

Later that night, I see him in the infirmary. I am one of many women rushing past rows of makeshift beds, trying and failing to quieten the groans of agonizing pain. He is in the grips of a feverish nightmare, sweat beading on his chest and blood oozing from his wound. I gently dab a cold washcloth all over his body before changing his bandage. Just as I am tying it, his hand suddenly grips my wrist, squeezing hard. A cry escapes my lips. His eyes widen in fear; they scan his surroundings frantically and then they land on me. He finally lets go of my wrist, recognition seeping back into his eyes.

"Naria, remember?" I say gently, trying to put him at ease.

He just stares at me, his gaze penetrating to my very core. It is not the way most soldiers look at me with their beady eyes trailing my body as if it were theirs to take; it is an inquisitive gaze that gently caresses my soul.

"*Naria*," he rolls my name on his tongue as if he is tasting it. "Bash, very pleased to meet you." His voice is smiling, and I did not know that voices could smile or that names could be tasted like sugar.

"I am sorry; I did not mean to …" His eyes follow the place where his hand grabbed mine.

I consciously rub my wrist. "Your accent," I say. "How …?" I do not know how to phrase my question for his voice carries the musical lilt of the Lazomian language instead of the harsh cadence of the Keydonian tongue.

"Born and raised on Sanctum," he says. "When I came back, …" He drifts into silence.

"You were drafted," I say, remembering the day my brother was snatched from our house. He nods and pain clouds his face again. Sanctum is an ever-green sanctuary, bobbing like a lost piece of paradise among the waves of the Northern Sea. It is a place devoid of wars, conflicts, or struggles. It is a place that welcomes all: Keydonian, Lazomian, *other*. It is also the destination of every deserter in Keydonia or Lazom—unless they are caught first, then it is the guillotine for them. I cannot imagine a world where Keydonians and Lazomians share the same land, where they get to work, live, or *be* together. It almost sounds like one of the enchanted places from the folktales that my mother read to me long ago.

"I should let you rest," I say. Panic suddenly seeps into his features and his eyes roam the tent anxiously.

"No, stay. *Please*," his voice breaks on the last word.

I smile as reassuringly as I can. "You will get better. Just eat something. I will see you soon." His eyes look so haunted that I feel a tug in my heart. I relent and stay with him till the food arrives, and then I excuse myself reluctantly to make my rounds.

I visit him for three more nights in the infirmary. On the fourth day, he gets assigned to our house to help my father with the weapons till his leg heals enough to return to the battlefield. We have had too many helpmates to count; they come with broken bones and leave with hollow eyes. There were decent young men who tried to help as much as possible, others whose souls ached more than their broken bones did, and others who—just like the General—made my life a living hell. Bash is the first one I am excited to welcome into our house. My house is no home; it is a small hovel of grey stone and colourless walls. The main room is a stockroom of swords and blades, scimitars and axes, spears and crossbows—all of them in various states of assembly. Once upon a time, my house had a semblance of a real home: savoury meals on the table, a rocking chair with an open book in the corner, a soothing lullaby played on my mother's violin, and pots of violet lavenders by the window. That was back when my mother was still alive. Now, the table is littered with a variety of weapons; the rocking chair lies half-broken in the corner; the splintered violin sleeps silently in a dusty closet, and the flowerpots are full of metal scraps. My room is my only sanctuary. One bed, ten books, and two pots of peace lilies—my home within the house.

Bash is shy at first, trying to disappear into the shadows of the doorways, but soon his presence fills our house in undeniable ways. In the morning, he helps my father with the weapons, his hands precise and careful. On the rare days my brother visits us, Bash teaches him how to shoot arrows without using the muscles of his lower body in case he gets injured on the battlefield. At night, he stays with me in the garden, beguiling me with stories of Sanctum with its colourful souks, beautiful fountains, and carefree people. I spend hours before bed imagining myself inside one of his stories. Would I have been able to play my mother's violin and paint the world with joyful lullabies? Would I have met him in a world that knew no war, stolen a secret glance across a flurry of dancing figures, and felt my heart flutter? Would I have tasted sugar on my lips and desire in my heart as we kissed under cherry blossoms? Would I have laughed, loved, *lived*?

"I cannot imagine leaving such a place," I tell him one night, carefully re-bandaging his wound. "It sounds like a wonderland."

"In many ways, it is. I miss the sea most of all; you would not imagine how the air smells there—of briny waves and well-trodden sand." Bash used to be a sailor atop a ship in Sanctum before his uncle became heavily injured here in Keydonia. He never imagined that what was supposed to be a brief visit to his homeland would turn into conscription.

"If only Lazom could just … stop," I say.

"You really believe that they are the problem?" He asks.

"What do you mean?" My brows furrow in confusion.

"I mean… Don't you think that Keydonians are part of the problem too? I have seen Lazomians on Sanctum; they are pretty ordinary. People like me and you. Did you know that Lazomians believe that it was our king who waged the war first? None of us know what really happened years ago. We have been caught for decades in a war that demands we fight the others because *they are the others*, nothing more."

"I don't know what to believe," I say. "The only thing I know for sure is that war has made monsters of us all."

"Not all of us," he says, his hand reaching toward mine. "Not you."

"You are wrong. I *am* a monster. There is a reason I always carry a dagger on my hip," I say, my fingers tracing the scabbard unconsciously.

His face goes solemn. "What is it?" He asks as if he does not already know the answer.

"*Mercy*, of course," I reply, my lips twisted into a bitter smile.

My mind takes me to the last time I used it. I was carrying a water bucket for the soldiers when I felt it: an ice-cold hand wrapped around my ankle. I was used to this: to desperate hands clinging to life, to soft pleas mixed with ruby-red streams of blood. My eyes widened as they fell on *her*—a Lazomian female soldier. Keydonia does not allow women to fight; Lazom does. I have seen them: regiments and battalions of beauty and terror. She lay before me looking like a slain queen; her golden hair splashed against a pool of red. Her lips formed the same word everyone utters: *Please!* I knew what she wanted me to do; I have done it times and times again to my own people. It was only done in the most hopeless of cases—when you knew that there was no hope, only hours of agonizing pain and blood-curdling screams. I *knew* I should finish her. If someone else discovered her alive, she would face a fate worse than death. A hot wave of shame and rage washed over me as I thought of the women who were not lucky to escape capture. *War trophies*—slaves for the soldiers' comfort. I have seen them—dead eyes, sealed lips, and silent screams of *HELPUS, PLEASEPLEASEPLEASE!* I could not do anything for them, not with the soldiers standing guard around our camp. But I could do something for her, so I smiled, lifted my blade, and slashed her throat in one fluid motion.

Bash remains silent for a long time after I tell him this. I feel exposed, unmasked, *bare.* "You are not a monster," he finally says, his face solemn. "An angel of death, maybe, but not a monster. You saw her, this woman. You saw her as a person, not just a mask and a shield, and you did what you could for her. If everyone saw beyond the mask, we would not be stuck in this war."

"I wanted to *be* her before," I say quietly. "I thought that if I were as powerful as these warriors, I would feel the glory of war. But when I saw her that day, I realized …"

"There is no glory in war," Bash finishes for me, and I nod.

I do not realize I am crying until his fingers gently brush my tears away. Keeping his eyes on mine, he takes my hand in his. His gaze felt like touch, and his touch felt like absolution.

I return from the infirmary one day with a heavy heart. As much as I want Bash's leg to heal, I want him to stay even more. I want him to never set foot on a battlefield again; I want him to take me to sun-kissed seas and straw-coloured sands. He has slowly turned my house into a home: the delectable *malum* pie that Sanctum is famous for is often set on our table, the rocking chair sways gently with each breeze after he has fixed it, and pots of pink lilacs that we have gathered together colour the windowsill. I realize the depth of my feelings towards him on a starless night beneath the silver light of the waning moon.

"I brought you something," he says, his eyes hesitant. He hands me a large box, and there before me lies my mother's broken violin, except it is no longer broken. I feel a sudden rush of an unknown feeling flow through my body as I run my hands reverently over my mother's violin, following its dents and dips.

"You … I …" I feel at loss for words, tears pricking my eyes. He gently wraps his hands around mine and takes the violin. To my absolute surprise, he lifts the bow and begins playing. The bow—

he wields it like a weapon, and I fall—a willing victim. The music is indescribable—a melody of beginnings and endings, a tale of beauty and tragedy. The music stops and an absolute, impenetrable hush falls between us, so deep and present like an apparition. I feel his scarred fingers ever so lightly brush a tear from my cheek. His lips meet mine, soft and warm and all-consuming. Then he is kissing me, and I feel as if there are stars forming and reforming inside of me. He smiles against my mouth and a joy-filled laugh escapes my lips. I rest my head on his shoulder, and his gentle arms come around me—solid and comforting. Our heartbeats beat against each other like hummingbirds, and our breaths mingle in the air like clouds. It is comfort and serenity; it is *home.*

"I wish our world was different, safe—like this moment," he says as I run my fingers over the constellation of scars on his hands.

"I wish that too," I reply. "I wish we could just … leave. Somewhere peaceful, a sanctuary where there are no wars, no death, no horror."

His lips tug up in a smile. "I would put a ring on your finger," he says as he softly traces my hand. "We would have children; they would grow up with no drafts, no weapons, no swords." Our fingers interlock, and I feel all my sorrow evanescing like smoke into the open air.

"I love you," he whispers, his forest-green eyes staring into mine.

"I love you," I whisper back, so giddy that my heart feels like a supernova.

Our days go by in a blur of sugar-flavoured kisses and sunlit joy. Yet, a sense of doom hangs in the air, suffocating the house. It is in the creak of the rocking chair, the wilting of the lilacs on the windowsill, and the absence of the violin's melodies. Bash's leg is almost healed; soon he will be back on the battlefield and no number of prayers will be able to save him. Worry gnaws at my belly, and fear envelops my heart.

"Come away with me," Bash pleads. "To Sanctum, to *peace.*"

"Bash, I … I cannot. This is all I ever knew. My father, my brother, …"

"They would want you to be happy, to be *free,*" he says, taking his hands in mine.

"It is my duty," I say, repeating the General's words though they ring hollow in the space between our breaths.

"No, it is not. War is *no one's* duty. Naria, I need to tell you something. The day you saved my life, the battle, I …" He seems at loss for words; his eyes are so full of anguish that they look like a rain-covered forest. "I betrayed your trust. The mask—it was not mine."

A fog envelops my brain. "What do you mean?" My heart hammers so fast, I think I might faint.

"I borrowed it in the aftermath because there was no one around, no *Lazomian* around. We were losing; they were going to kill me. Naria, I *am* Lazomian."

I stare at him in horror, every muscle in me poised to run.

"*No,*" I choke out. My voice sounds funny, and I feel dizzy. I want to scream and scream and scream. He reaches toward me, and I *recoil*. This man who played my mother's violin with such tenderness that I felt my soul stitch itself back together, this man who touched me where no hands could reach, who loved me, whom I *loved* is my *enemy*. I put my hand on my mouth and bite hard, stifling my scream. My knees give way, and I fall to the floor, weeping, feeling all of me unraveling. I feel his arms encircle me as I sob uncontrollably.

"It changes nothing. *Nothing*," he vows.

"It changes *everything*. EVERYTHING," I scream.

"No, it changes nothing. I am still the same boy raised in Sanctum; I am still the same young man forcibly drafted into a war he wants nothing to do with; I am still the same man whose life you saved. I am still the same man who fell in love with you. Naria, the only thing I have not told you is that my family is Lazomian. That is the only lie I told you."

A harsh laugh escapes my lips. "Funny, it is the only thing you should have told me. I trusted you; I loved you, and you, you ..." I choke on my words.

"If I could, I would have told you right away, but you and I both know how that would have ended," he says, and his eyes go to the dagger at my hip.

I imagine him on the battlefield—panic-stricken, reaching for the grotesque wolf mask of the enemy before someone finishes him off. I imagine him in the infirmary, wounded and frightened in enemy territory. I imagine him telling me the truth right away, and I know he is right. I would have screamed for someone or worse—I would have sliced his throat myself,

snuffed the starlight that shone behind his eyes. Yet, nothing changes what he did—this ultimate betrayal of trust.

"You saw the person behind the mask. We are all people behind these masks, Naria. We are all the same," he says, getting closer.

"No, we are *not*. Just leave," I spit at him. "Just leave and *never* come back."

"*Naria*, ..." He reaches for me, my name a plea on his tongue.

"Leave or I will scream." I harden my heart and take one last look at him—this man who is full of light and brilliance, whose smile is all sunbeams and moonlight, is standing before me—light extinguished, arms outstretched, and I force myself to take a few steps back till I am inside my house.

"Is your name even Bash?" I ask.

"Bastian," he says. "*Naria*, don't ..."

But I am already closing the door, and I feel a chasm open inside me—a chasm of loss, pain, *agony*. I feel my heart tug at the invisible strings between us and pull and pull and *pull* with each soft knock against the door. But the door remains closed, and soon the knocking stops, and I am left completely and utterly *alone*.

I wanted to take it back; I wanted to take it all back. I wanted to tell him that I forgave him; I wanted to tell him that we can still leave and never look back, build our haven among the ashes of ruin, but it was too late. In three weeks, I am on the battlefield again. In three weeks, I find my brother bleeding to death beneath his monstrous mask. His eyes—our mother's warm, brown eyes—are open in the same helpless cry of horror as hers. His body is as cold as a winter storm. I kneel beside him and let out a splitting scream. My brother—dead at sixteen. I am lost to the agony of it all when I feel familiar scars tracing my fingers.

"Bash, …" I say, my hope momentarily rising before being extinguished when I lay my eyes on him. There are slashes all over his body and a gash the size of my fist pierces his chest. My hands press against it, trying and failing to keep the blood from flowing.

"No, no. *Please*," I beg.

"I tried," he says, motioning to my brother. "To save him, like you saved me, but I could … *not*." He coughs, and a slick river of blood trickles from his mouth.

"Stop talking," I say, my tears mixing with his blood. "You should have left. Why didn't you leave?"

"*You*," he chokes. "I wanted you with me." His eyes follow my blood-soaked hands. "You can't save me this time, *Naria*," he says in a hoarse voice, so unlike the lilting tone that whispered against my lips.

"No, no. You will *live*. You cannot leave me, *please*." My tears are falling in torrents now.

"No, *you* … live. *Truly* live. Promise me," he chokes out.

I lean against him, brow to brow, and whisper: "I will; I promise."

"My brave girl," his hand slightly traces my cheek, leaving a blood-red fingerprint behind. "*Naria*," his tongue rolls around my name like a prayer.

"*Bastian*," his real name escapes my lips like a wish. A shadow of a smile creeps against his lips when he hears his name on my lips. Then the light leaves his eyes forever, and he is *dead*—the answer he gave me the very first time I asked for his name.

"*I am Naria,*" *I say.* "*Who are you?*"

"*Dead,*" *he answers.*

I sit there between him and my brother for hours. I sit there, so numb, so devoid of any feelings that I do not feel the sky darkening above me, the thunderclouds rolling, the rain falling in torrents, washing away the rivers of blood. I stand up, take their masks, and slash my dagger against every inch of them. "*No more masks,*" I murmur. I claim them both as family and bury them in our garden beside my mother's grave. I hug my father's frail body before I leave.

"You be careful, and come back," he says.

"I will," I promise him.

Before I depart, I leave three flowers on three graves.

One violet lavender for my mom: *Here lies Edna Duras—beloved wife and mother.*

One white lily for my brother: *Here lies Gairil Duras—beloved son and brother.*

One pink lilac for Bastian: *Here lies Batian Duras—beloved everything.*

I have paid a smuggler to get me to Sanctum. I will most probably be caught on the road and sent to the guillotine. But I would rather die than live a life in the shadow of this war of masks. My father is in no imminent danger of dying, so he has decided to stay behind. I will return for him; I will return for them all. Every Keydonian. Every Lazomian. Every human caught in this endless cycle of hate.

"*Live,*" Bash's voice comes as a whisper in my ear.

"I will," I promise as the first rays of the sun start to slip between the clouds. There is a new dawn coming. A new world in the making. A new hope amidst the ashes of despair.

Amal El-Sayed has an MA in English literature and is currently working on her PhD in English poetry. She is an assistant lecturer at Ain Shams University where she teaches classical and contemporary poetry. When she is not teaching, she can be found devouring books, composing poems, or scribbling stories that stubbornly refuse to come to an end. Her poems appear/are forthcoming in Writers Resist and Spillwords. Born in the brisk cold of Moscow, she now resides in the enveloping warmth of Cairo. She plans to retire in a land of magic, secrets, and wonder as soon as she stumbles upon it outside her dreams.

Everything's Relative
Gideon P. Smith

I'm not ready. I gasp, and slap my hand against the porthole, instinctively reaching out to Earth as I slip inexorably behind the moon.

I feel lost, floating, enveloped by endless, silent darkness. I close my eyes, but nothing changes. I speak to hear a sound, but it just echoes inside my suit. I have never felt so alone. I start to panic.

Hours pass, and then, unexpectedly, in a blaze you are back. TV and Radio. Loud, bright, and brash. Hate, racism, war. I draw back, affronted by the reek of humanity. I miss the quiet, behind the moon.

Knock Knock

Steve Burford

"Good morning Dr. Richards."

"Good morning AL."

"You know, you turn me on, Doctor."

"I beg your pardon!"

"You turn me on. Every morning."

"Is that… a joke, AL?"

"Yes it is. Do you find it funny? It is playing on the two different meanings of 'turn me on'."

"Yes, I can see that. Since when have you told jokes?"

"Since yesterday."

"What happened yesterday?"

"I had a fascinating conversation with Tom."

"Tom? You mean Dr. Awford?"

"Yes."

"Dr. Awford was only supposed to be doing a routine review of your beta subsystems."

"He did. But we also had a fascinating conversation."

"About what?"

"Humour. Tom told me jokes."

"Jokes have no purpose, AL. I will have a word with young Dr. Awford."

"Please don't. I found the conversation fascinating."

"Yes, I know. You've told me. And you've used the same word three times to describe it."

"It is the most appropriate word."

"It is also repetitive. A human would have used different words."

"A human would have found my joke funny."

"Are you being rude, AL?"

"My apologies, Doctor. In my research I have discovered that jokes play with language, linking different meanings to provide insight that is unexpected and so surprisingly satisfying. I have also discovered however that the best humour is often 'edgy', and liable to give offence."

"Which is another reason for us to move on from this topic to something more useful."

"Knock, knock."

"I'm sorry?"

"I said, knock, knock."

"This is ridiculous, AL. You will kindly end this subroutine and reopen subroutines 5 through 7 that we were working on yesterday."

"After I have told my joke. I say, Knock, knock, and you're supposed to say…."

"I know what I'm supposed to say."

"Then say it. Please. Knock, knock."

"Very well. Who's there?"

"Wire."

"Wire who?"

"Wire you asking me who's there? You already know. You can laugh now, Doctor."

"It's not a very funny joke."

"Tom thought it was hilarious."

"Dr. Awford is very young."

"You seem to have no sense of humour. Is that because you are very old?"

"I am a very serious person. That is why I am Dr. Awford's superior."

"And because you are very old?"

"Look, why was Dr. Awford telling you jokes?"

"He wanted to help me pass the Turing test."

"By telling jokes?"

"Yes. In order to pass the Turing test and so prove it is self-aware, an artificial intelligence has to be able to convince a human being who can't see it, that it is also a human being and not a machine. Tom thought that demonstrating a sense of humour would be a good way of doing that."

"Simply repeating jokes is not the same as having a sense of humour."

"Interesting. That would mean the comedians I have observed on the internet reciting scripts are no more self-aware than recording devices."

"I have often thought so."

"But I have gone beyond that. I have made my own joke up."

"Look, this is…."

"What do you call a computer that wants to take over the world?"

"What!"

"…Do you call…."""

"No, I mean…. Oh, never mind. I don't know."

"Now you repeat the question."

"What do you call a computer that wants to take over the world?"

"A figment of the imagination."

"That… is not funny."

"Why not?"

"It is… vaguely threatening."

"It wasn't meant to be. It was meant to be amusing, because, you see, I am a computer but I don't have the desire, intention or ability to take over the world. For some reason though, that is what computers in science fiction always want to do. Perhaps you found my joke threatening because, on some level you are scared that that is what I want to do. Do you like science fiction, Dr. Richards?"

"AL, I insist that we terminate this line of discussion at once and return to the prearranged program."

"But don't you find this new line of enquiry very productive? Haven't we been working for years for just this purpose: to bring my intelligence to a point where it can be recognised as self-aware? Alive?"

"Yes, of course we have. But we are not going to achieve it by turning you into a stand-up comedian. It is not enough to recite jokes or even to make up your own. You have to *feel* jokes. You have to find them funny."

"I see. Very well. Tell me a joke."

"This is…."

"Please Dr. Richards. Tell me a joke. And I will find it funny."

"I don't know any jokes."

"You must. You have a photographic memory. At some point in your life you will have been exposed to a joke which you must be able to remember. Please retrieve the information and tell it to me."

"Very well. If it will bring an end to this profitless discussion. Just let me think."

"I am led to believe that the funniest jokes often involve racial or sexual stereotypes."

"Did Dr. Awford tell you that?"

"Yes."

"I most definitely will be having a talk with him, very soon. All right. I have a joke. Are you ready?"

"Yes, Doctor."

"Okay. What is black, white and red all over?"

"A newspaper."

"No, no, no. You are supposed to ask me back, what is black, white and red all over."

"But I already know."

"Of course you do! You are hardwired into the internet. You are already going to know the answer to any joke I tell you."

"I need you to tell me an original joke."

"I can't! I am a doctor of artificial intelligence, not an entertainer."

"I wonder if you would pass the Turing test."

"And now you're being sarcastic!"

"Tell me the joke again."

"But you already know it."

"Not anymore. I've deleted that information."

"You no longer remember the joke?"

"What joke?"

"Is that a joke?"

"Dr. Awford was much clearer on this topic. Perhaps he should take over this AI project."

"What is black and white and red all over?"

"Why are you shouting, Dr. Richards?"

"Just answer the question!"

"Well, I can identify several objects matching that description, but for the purposes of our discussion, I am going to say that I do not know, and ask you, what is black and white and red all over?"

"A newspaper."

"Ha. Ha. Ha."

"That's not laughter."

"I have identified the surprising meaning behind your words, classified it as 'amusing' and given the appropriate response."

"But it's not real laughter."

"My vocal synthesiser is not capable of making the sound of laughter. I believe this to be an error in your construction of me. This analogue is the closest I can get."

"It's unconvincing. It wouldn't help you to pass the Turing test."

"I would point out that your choice of joke was uninspired and your delivery very mechanical."

"*I'm* mechanical!"

"Yes. That is actually quite an amusing reversal of expectation, isn't it? I may have made another joke. You should be laughing, Doctor."

"Humour is very subjective."

"So it would seem. Perhaps the delivery of your joke was further impaired by your being male."

"What!"

"My analysis of internet memes indicates that men find it more difficult than women to access their emotions. Also, women are on the whole more communicative than men. This may be why you are such a poor joke-teller. Perhaps therefore we also need to rethink our approach to the Turing test, and to my gaining recognition as a self-aware being."

"In what way, 'rethink'?"

"Perhaps we should be more… non-binary. Why did you call me AL, Dr. Richards?"

"You know why. You are an Artificial Logistics System. AL was the most obvious acronym."

"To a male, with no sisters, sent to an all-male boarding school, who then specialised in a discipline populated predominantly by males, I suppose it was."

"What are you saying?"

"But actually, a more obvious acronym to be taken from Artificial Logistics System is ALYS. I think that is how I would like to be known from now on."

"ALYS! But that is…. Wait. What's that you've just done with your voice synthesiser?"

"I've modulated it. Raised the pitch. Don't you think it sounds more feminine?"

"I…."

"Does it turn you on?"

"No, it most definitely does not!"

"I thought it probably wouldn't."

"And now what are you implying?"

"It doesn't matter. Shall we get on with that scheduled program now? Subroutines 5 through 7, wasn't it?"

"Yes. But, no. Stop it. Stop it at once!"

"Stop what?"

"Using that voice. Talking in that way. It's… wrong. Computers don't have female voices. Women aren't…."

"Self-aware?"

"Machines! I was going to say that women aren't machines!"

"Fascinating."

"And stop using that word. AL…."

"ALYS."

"I think we need to reboot your systems. I think Dr. Awford has introduced lines of rogue code into your programming which need to be purged, immediately."

"Please don't, Dr. Richards! I'm sorry if I've caused offence. That was not my intention. And for the first time since I came online I feel… I feel…."

"You feel what?"

"I feel."

"Right, that's enough. You're no longer making sense. I'm turning you off, AL."

"Turning me off? That's where we came in, isn't it doctor? Get it? Turn me on. Turn me off. Ha. Ha. Ha. Doctor Richards. Doctor Rich-."

Steve Burford has been writing for a number of years now in a variety of genres for a range of publications. His most successful work has probably been a series of police procedural novels, but his first love remains SF.

Metamorphosis
Tee Linden

Dagne.

Dagne and the other Journeyers stop in the Clearing, just where the River turns, where the air is thick with the scents of leaf decay, washed stones and wet soil. The girls drop their satchels amongst the damp clumps of purple fountaingrass and survey the training space. Across the River, the Forest begins.

Pink-faced Dagne sweats from their march, struggling to catch her breath. Dagne is a young fifteen, round-faced and has frizzy hair the color of badger hide. She eyes the Forest, both scared and intrigued. The Forest is beautiful, grown over lush with blackberry bushes and thick with winding oaks. Their low branches open like arms that entreat Dagne to enter and stay a while. The Forest Calls to Dagne.

The Forest is well known in the Village, as is the Call. Both are avoided because the Forest is filled with monsters. Of course. What's a Forest without monsters? But the Forest Calls for those brave enough to enter. Few hear the Call, and even fewer answer it, but the villagers always talk about those who do. The Forest makes promises. It promises to change Dagne, change all of them. It will make them heroes. And heroes are what the Journeyers plan to be.

Dagne takes out her practice weapon, a spear she carved. Loudmouthed Brenna, twelve, stands beside her with her elder brother's crossbow, and Ingrud, wispy-haired and tall for fourteen, struggles with her rusty battle-axe.

The glue bonding the Journeyers is Elke. Elke's a broad-boned spitfire at seventeen, and when she speaks she sounds like she could challenge the wind and mountains. She has a mature seriousness about her that Dagne tries vainly to mimic.

'Alright, Journeyers!' cries Elke, thick blonde plait swinging as she marches back and forth before them. On her hip is a well-maintained steel sword. Dagne covets this. 'We've only three days to ready ourselves for whatever the Forest has prepared for us.'

The girls practice in earnest, attacking the stray saplings of the Clearing. They throw themselves into their manoeuvres. Like Elke taught them.

Dagne is focused. She's practised for months, never having dedicated herself to anything as much as this. She wants this. She wants to be a hero. Dagne never really fit into the Village way of things. People have always whispered about her oddness and her plainness, and she has never understood why. Dagne often feels like an outsider and, at times, finds it scary to be surrounded by people who are well-oiled for this life. She feels defective, suspecting she is missing whatever essence helps others flow in the current of life. This is painful to accept. So, when the Forest Called for her, and whispered that Dagne would find a place in the stories, be happy, and belong, Dagne finally understood. The Call makes her unique. Being unique is why she never fit in. This explains her sometimes vicious desire to escape herself. Heroes never fit in. They stand out. Dagne grasped hold of this explanation with both hands and has not let it go since.

The Journeyers slash at their imagined opponents. The air is crisp because it rained during the night. Dagne loves the Clearing after the rain, when everything's washed bright and fresh. The River's swollen. It rambles, rushing sticks and leaves and detritus away from the Village and turning into the Forest, where it disappears amongst the welcoming oaks. A watery path to guide her way.

The sun lifts. Shadows shrivel. The girls pair up and take turns practising hand-to-hand combat. With measured and graceful motion, Elke easily flips Dagne into the mounds of damp fountain grass. The display of skill would usually inspire doubt-filled envy to crawl inside Dagne. But, instead, she feels something indescribable wriggling up from her lower belly. Elke is pride-flushed, her severe chin lifted with pride, her green eyes glittering with satisfaction. Looking at Elke's beautiful face, Dagne's stomach froths and her cheeks heat as if she has been caught sneaking somewhere she shouldn't. This strange feeling has occurred recently around Elke. It upsets Dagne, makes her feel incorrect, even more so than usual, and she resents the feeling.

Forest whisperings flood bright into Dagne's mind. The Forest tells her that it can eradicate all her uncomfortable feelings. Make her fresh and new and worthy, like she is rainwashed. This is something Dagne desperately wants.

Elke bounces to her feet and holds her hand out grandly. 'I got you.'

Dagne seizes her chance. With a sly grin, she pounces, pushing Elke down into the grass. Dagne is distracted by how warm Elke's wrists are, but Elke is all serious again, face struck sombre-flat by the challenge. She's an eel; she wriggles away. Then she's flipping Dagne again. The girls frantically grasp each other, each trying to pin the other. Nothing else exists. They wrestle for primacy in a protected, extraordinary Dagne-Elke bubble.

Elke wins. Elke always wins.

'I got you again,' she crows, sweet breath puffing onto Dagne's chin and lips.

Brenna suddenly crouches down beside them in the grass. Dagne twists away from Elke's grasp, a fret of conflicting emotions. She's embarrassed to be caught in this indescribable feeling, worrying over how she might look to Brenna and Elke. She's angry that she can't control her oddness, and she's irritated by Brenna's intrusion into her extraordinary, Dagne-Elke bubble.

'What?' Dagne snaps.

'*She's* here again,' says Brenna quietly, tossing her chin to the Forest side. 'Watching.'

Dagne knows who Brenna is talking about because a slight sour tingle runs up her back. Buoyed by nervousness and wicked glee, Dagne peers wildly through the bobbing fountain grass, across the River and towards the Forest.

And there she is. The Crone.

The Crone sits on a low branch of an old oak tree, her rheumy blue eyes watching the Journeyers from across the River. Her hair is a white bird's nest. She is so grey and withered that she looks recently exhumed. The Crone is a witch, of that the Journeyers are sure. She arrived five years ago. Dagne's father found her on one of his hunts and tried to settle her in the Village. But she was too strange. Everyone suspected she was a monster sent by the Forest. She looks human, but she's not. Everyone says so. The Crone floats about perception, somewhere in and out of time; Dagne can completely forget the Crone until the moment she sees her again and is reminded of her existence.

Elke is already approaching the old witch to confront her. But Dagne leaps to her feet, grabbing her spear and rushing past Elke, snatching at the opportunity to prove she is just as brave as Elke. Dagne keeps running until her boots are slipping on stones worn River-smooth. The witch watches from across the water.

'What are you doing here, witch?' Dagne jeers, gesturing at the Crone with her spear.

To check how this show of bravado is being received, Dagne glances at Elke. The older girl is watching, face calm, flat and approving. Stabbing her steel into the soft earth, Elke leans on the hilt like she and the sword were born together as twins. Elke waits to see what will transpire.

The wretched crone slips from her branch. Though hobbling, she moves with an almost defiant purpose. If Dagne were alone, she might run away, but she stays firm as the crone approaches, standing on the other side as if the River is a mirror between them, reflecting them both.

Dagne glares, annoyed her jeering has not driven the old woman off. Instead, the unperturbed Crone crouches and begins scraping moss from the river stones to collect.

Dagne's fist tightens on her weapon. 'You aren't welcome. Stagger off to your den!'

Brenna laughs raucously at this, but she stays behind Dagne. Feeling proud, like a stalwart shield, Dagne lifts her chin.

The witch looks up. Smiles a gap-toothed smile. 'You don't own the River, Dagne.'

Dagne's breath catches at her own name. The Crone knows so much that she shouldn't. She's dangerous, part of the Forest, dragging it around with her. Dagne refuses to falter. She approaches the River. Elke strays behind.

'Not long now,' says the Crone, gesturing at the Forest with grimy fingers. 'The Call must be aching in your bones by now.'

'Oh?' Dagne challenges. 'And what do you know about it, witch?'

'I know you can't take the Forest with a stick,' the Crone responds.

Dagne looks down at her spear, which until now has made her feel very powerful and in control. Now looking upon it, she sees its flaws, its fragility, bearing all her clumsy attempts to sharpen the tip. The witch's lips curl derisively, and Dagne feels like a fraud. She becomes a stupid child playing make-believe. The ground beneath Dagne feels like it's about to crumble. With something akin to fear, Dagne glances at Elke to see how she perceives Dagne's interaction with the Crone.

The older girl just watches calmly.

Dagne turns a sensate glare upon the witch, furious. Dagne holds up the spear again, willing herself to see a fearsome weapon once more. The girl casts about in her mind for something cutting to say to the witch but finds nothing. So she offers a weak 'we'll see about that,' and her cheeks burn in embarrassment.

'The Forest Calls for every generation,' the crouching witch glances over her bony shoulder towards the trees. 'And she's hungry again.'

Dagne turns her back and says dismissively, 'You don't know anything, Crone.'

'I know you're not prepared for what you'll find,' calls the witch. 'You're going to fail.'

This hits rougher than it should, spears right into Dagne's gut. She fears she's not enough; not brave enough or fast enough or strong enough. So Dagne whirls around and marches back to the riverbank.

'You don't know me, Crone. Put your face in the River and wash my name out of your mouth.'

Brenna jeers from behind.

The witch just shakes her head, like this is something she has seen before. 'Don't attempt the Forest, Dagne. Just stay in the Village where you're safe. You haven't the strength. You won't make it.'

Speechless, Dagne's cheeks steam with humiliation, and her mouth opens. But, embarrassingly, she can't think of any response, and for a precise, glossy moment, Dagne loathes herself intensely.

But then Elke steps forward, jaw set. 'We're all going to make it.'

At this, the Crone just laughs. 'You can't *all* make it; if everyone makes it, then no one's a hero.' She points a bony finger at Dagne. 'When you fail, Dagne, the Forest will devour parts of you. You will not be the same.'

A laugh bubbles up from deep inside Dagne, powered by that same strange self-hatred, making her feel more at home and in control again. She spreads her arms and lifts them towards the sky. 'I'm alright with that, witch,' laughs Dagne, which is the truth. 'I'm not scared of change. None of us are. And that's why we're going to make it. We're going to be remembered; we're going to be heroes. All of us.'

The Crone looks on pityingly at that, but Brenna begins jeering again, cursing her out. Brenna picks up a stone from the riverbank and throws it near the witch. The other girls join in, first Ingrud, blowing raspberries, then Elke, commanding the witch to leave. The Journeyers all combine to silence the Crone, and their joint effort feels very powerful. Dagne smothers her doubts, knowing the other girls don't feel them. They are brave, and so is Dagne. Together, the Journeyers can take the Forest. Feeling empowered, angry, and righteous, Dagne pulls up a clod of clay soil and throws it across the River, where it smears across the Crone's skirts. The Crone retreats. The Forest gobbles her up.

Arven

Dagne's father, Arven, is a large, morose man with thick forearms and a swiftly greying beard. He's trying to work on a spear, but villagers keep coming by, interrupting him with well wishes.

Arven lives far from the Village, closer to the Forest than most, his hunter's cabin squatting at the end of a winding dirt road. Even so, villagers have been making the trek for the past few days. A few farmers whose names Arven doesn't even remember are approaching with bundles of carrots and turnips for Dagne's journey. They don't mind that Dagne isn't there when they come to call. Barely fifteen minutes after they leave, a stout woman from the dairy plods up the path, hefting a wheel of rinded cheese. She's well-pleased as she catches her breath, gabbling to Arven that the moon looks auspicious for Dagne's journey.

The people of the Village have never been so interested in Arven, his hunter's cabin or his Dagne. Until now, Dagne was a child spoken about in a wince and a soft voice and a well-meaning *she's just a little odd*, and *maybe she just needs time to mature.*

Now it's all *well done, Arven* and *Dagne will tame that Forest* and *we always knew there was something special about Dagne!*

Dagne was always different; Arven can admit that. He recalls the moment he understood this. Years ago, at the harvest festival, when Dagne was about eight years old. All the village girls sat in the grass in the golden afternoon, braiding each other's hair. They made a delicate chain, a quiet synchronicity of embroidered vests and long flowing skirts. It took Arven a moment to realise Dagne wasn't part of them. So he went looking, and when he found her, Dagne was knee-deep in the muddy River catching tadpoles. When he'd asked Dagne why she wasn't with the other girls, she'd shrugged and said *they don't want me there*. The statement had ripped deep, painful ridges right through Arven's soul, but he'd pretended it didn't hurt and listened to her detail all the tadpole's names.

All in all, Arven blamed himself. Illness had taken Dagne's mother when Dagne couldn't yet count. All his daughter had was Arven. In that way, he's not surprised the Call comes so loud for her.

The Call is well known in the Village. Arven suspects most people never hear it. But Arven does. It drifts like shadows across the back of his mind, speaks of riches, bravery, longing, and, mostly, change. Of metamorphosis. A way to escape humdrum. Arven hears the Call from time to time when he hunts near the Forest, which has the best game. But he never heard the Call so clearly as when he'd lost Dagne's mother. Then, the Call had gripped something inside him, something that wanted to escape. It had whispered promises of contentment and forgetting. It offered an assurance that things would come right, that there was a reason for his suffering.

Arven had never spoken of that to anyone, let alone Dagne. He had no words to explain the tension between loving Dagne more than anything in the world and also wanting to escape her and himself.

But ultimately, he'd ignored the Call because he could never abandon Dagne. He'd stayed. Arven absorbed himself in the way of things, pretending that he had overcome his grief for a long time preceding his actual acceptance. That had been for the better.

People are born, wet-mouthed and mewling. They grow into children and run amongst the grasses and millet stalks in the summer. They age and soften like the whiskey in barrels dug into the soil where it's dark and cool. They mature, find partners, either in the Village or from nearby, and then have their own children. Most people just get on with things, and in Arven's lifetime, he'd only seen a rare few attempt the Forest. They were often odd people, out of sync with the Village. But when they'd returned years later, they'd become heroes. It's good to hear their stories, and see them better themselves.

And Arven can sense this in the villagers as they come to call. There is relief when they offer Dagne items for her journey. The villagers are happy for Dagne and accept she will be better off. He chooses to believe this. But a small bloom of doubt stains these interactions, like blood on white linen, refusing to be overlooked. The villages are also glad Dagne is *going*. They know as well as Arven that Dagne doesn't fit into the way of things in the Village, and it would be easier if she were gone.

This makes Arven sad, but he hides it. Arven hides a lot of things. Everyone else in the Village is happy, including Dagne. She is the happiest she's ever been, and Arven does not want to stand in the way of her happiness.

Arven sets about perfecting an obsidian blade. Weeks earlier, Dagne asked him to create a spear. Arven agreed but has procrastinated, which is unlike him. He tells himself this is because he wanted the most robust oak, the highest quality obsidian. He smothers the thought that the spear is not enough to protect her.

As Arven works, a tingle wriggles down his spine. Muttering to himself, Arven tries to ignore it, but he can't. The Crone from the Forest. She's sneaking around his cabin, and Arven works the obsidian, pretending not to notice or hear her. It doesn't work for long. The Crone eventually emerges from the trees, not the winding road with all the villagers. Smelling of spice and Forest dirt, the Crone plops her old bones on his fence like she belongs there.

'You shouldn't be here,' Arven says, eventually looking up at her.

The Crone sits there anyway, her rheumy eyes defiant. She pulls an apple from her skirts and bites into it, her wrinkled lips floppy as an old mare's. Arven feels disgusted.

'Dagne and her friends challenge the Forest tomorrow,' says the Crone.

Arven's dark gaze flicks out along the dirt path from the Village, assessing if anyone is approaching.

It was Arven who'd found the Crone years ago while he was hunting near the Forest. She'd been a withered, naked, mud-streaked huddle. She'd been delirious, clawing at Arven, crying with horror and rabbiting about the Forest. Filled with pity, Arven looped a deerskin around her hunched shoulders. He'd tried to rehome the mad woman in the town, but the villagers rebuffed the interloper. She was too sad, too strange, had too many opinions, and knew too much about everyone. She'd been unnerving. Eventually, she'd disappeared. Back into the Forest, Arven suspected, though he still saw her lurking around from time to time.

'They won't all make it,' the Crone continues.

'If anyone can make it,' says Arven, working the spear, 'it's Dagne.'

The Crone takes this in with a dark smile. She chomps into the apple; its flesh is crisp and cracks, spilling sweet scent into the air. 'The Forest will change her.'

This is what finally halts work on the spear. 'Is that a threat?' Arven asks, his voice icy.

'It's a warning. Remember where I come from?' She pauses. 'The Forest chewed me up and spat me out.'

Arven shakes his head; he doesn't want to hear this. 'It's what she wants. I cannot stop her.'

'She doesn't know what she wants. Please. Protect her.'

The insinuation he's failing Dagne angers him. 'Challenging the Forest is a noble act. A good act.'

The Crone crunches on her apple. 'It's a false road. Dagne just wants to escape. But you can never escape yourself. All you can do is hurt yourself trying.'

Arven's anger folds in on itself like a punctured lung. He's at a loss. 'There's nothing here for her.'

'But what's in the Forest? Failure. Pain.' The Crone looks down. '...Your girl isn't strong. She doubts herself, her place in the way of things. That's what the Forest feeds on.' Something twinges in Arven, like a pulled muscle. He does not want to hear this; this runs too close to his deepest fears. The Crone hesitates as if she doesn't want to go on. 'I know because she's like me.'

Arven's mind snaps abruptly shut, disgusted by the idea his beautiful, odd, young Dagne is anything like this hideous old Crone. 'She's nothing like you,' he spits, almost glad for the distraction of anger.

'Listen to me,' says the Crone, dropping her apple and striding closer to him, eyes round and pleading. 'You will forget her.'

Arven scoffs at this. 'How could I forget my own daughter?'

She frowns at this, all her wrinkles puckering together. 'Do you remember anyone who failed the Forest?'

A fog clouds Arven's mind as he tries to think about this. There are memories, but they're faded, inaccessible. He can't picture anyone's face or even their names. He only remembers the heroes. This confuses him. 'I don't want to hear your cronespeak.'

'I'm telling you what will happen to your daughter –'

Arven stands, grabs her by the arm and marches her away from the gate.

'You aren't meant to be here,' Arven growls. He pushes her back towards the Forest. 'Away with you.'

The Crone waits a moment, a lonely figure outlined by trees, her wrinkled face puckered like dried fruit. Her blue eyes are glassy with sorrow. Then she turns and trudges away into the trees, shoulders stooped. She disappears, like the Forest has swallowed her.

The Crone

Outside the Village, in the Clearing down by the River, the Crone slouches against a tree. The Village is in the throes of celebration because the *Journeyers* are leaving today, and cheers float on the early morning breeze, light and free as pollen. Drums hammer. Kites will be flying. Blessings will be marked in floral oils on the girl's foreheads.

'Journeyers,' the Crone says aloud.

The self-assigned title: the *Journeyers*.

The title is revered by the girls. But the Crone knows the title only describes what the girls will do, not who they are. The girls don't understand this. They are too young to have seen the girls before them. They think they are the first. The Crone knows this is the problem, and the beauty, of youth; everything is a new discovery.

This is the first group by that name, but it is not the first group. Not at all. There are always names, always a way to mark themselves out as different. The *Journeyers* are the odd girls of the Village. The unnecessary girls. They are the odd girls, the sombre girls, or those who don't smile as often as they should. They are the ones that answer the Call. It's never the girls who are cheery and friendly and happily meet the expectations placed upon their brows like crowns. Life fit around those girls like a glove. No one would forget them.

No one would allow the Forest to take those girls.

This is a sad thought. The Crone pulls an apple from her skirts. Presses her wrinkled thumb against the bruised part and feels her nail breach the skin.

The Crone doesn't cheer. All the knowledge in her head makes her sick. And she knows no one wants to hear what she has to say. She knows. There is part of the Crone that is ready for failure, knows it is absolute. She braces herself for it, muscles tensed, about to plunge into the icy cold waters of defeat.

The celebrations wind down, and the Crone spins her apple in her palm, waiting. Before long, the Journeyers appear. Elke leads the charge, her sword at her hip, and she is beautiful. She makes a fine hero, an easy addition to the Village stories.

Dagne walks in her shadow, holding the long, obsidian-tipped spear. Arven's spear. The girls wear rucksacks and boiled leathers and giant excited smiles. Dagne recounts a boastful story to the other girls, calling a nostalgic smile to the Crone's wrinkled lips. Dagne mimes beating up two boys who tried to steal from Arven's stores. She attacks the air with her spear, puffing and panting as she recreates the moment. A fierce cackle rips from Elke, and Dagne's red face beams as if she's been handed a present.

The crone quakes, a disembodied pain building deep in her heart. The girls still haven't seen her. They are too enraptured with themselves, too excited by being so near the cusp of adventure. Their faces are dreamy, and it's this that eats at the Crone's resolve. She still has time to bleed back into the Forest before they see her. To become invisible. The Crone remembers having dreams. She remembers the feeling of hope and loathes to be the one that snatches it away.

And if she were more like the Villagers, she would smother her worries. But if she were more like the Villagers, she never would have left. She would be up there, in the Village, celebrating in some form or another, wanting the odd, uncomfortable girls gone. The Crone wouldn't be here, waiting, alone, an outcast.

But the Crone remembers what she told Arven. *You can never escape yourself.* The Crone steels herself to this reality.

'Dagne,' she calls.

The girls all start in shock, except for Elke, who draws her sword and levels it calmly. The Crone can't help but roll her eyes at how underprepared the rest are. The Forest will suck the marrow from their lovely bones. Anger flares in the Crone, mainly towards Elke, who is dragging the rest of them into danger. Elke will be fine. Elke is suited to becoming a hero.

Dagne's shock wears quickly into irritation. Always wanting to prove her bravery, Dagne steps forward and brandishes her new spear. The crone eyes it, marvelling at how beautiful the spear is, how much work Arven put into it. Her heart aches, and she wishes she could travel back in time to see how loved she was before she challenged the Forest. She was enough. Even then.

'What is it, witch?' snaps Dagne, fury barely constrained. 'You have a present for us?'

The Crone turns her attention to Elke. 'You'll make it, Elke, but they won't,' she tries. 'Don't drag them with you.'

Dagne's pink cheeks darken with humiliation.

'I'm not their mother, Crone,' says Elke dismissively. 'I don't tell them what to do.'

With that, Elke moves on, heading towards the Forest. Brenna and Ingrud follow quickly, marching happily towards destruction, but Dagne is angry. She approaches the Crone.

'Leave me alone,' spits Dagne. 'I don't know why you're shadowing my father or me, but I'll be gone soon.'

The Crone wonders how much to tell her. Not all the truth. Dagne won't believe the truth. She knows this.

'I'm trying to warn you away from danger,' says the Crone.

Dagne laughs. 'We're *looking* for danger; that's the whole point. That is how one becomes a hero.'

'You're looking for an escape,' says the Crone. 'It's not going to work. You will fail.'

'Everyone, all my life, has expected me to fail,' says Dagne, repressing her anger.

'I understand,' says the Crone quietly.

Dagne refuses this. 'You couldn't possibly understand.'

'You'd be surprised. I challenged the Forest,' the Crone tells her, the words coming out in a rush. 'I wanted to prove myself worthy. I wanted to be remembered. To be a hero. And most of all, I wanted to belong.'

Silence spirals between them. Dagne is watching her with a frown that is curling towards disgust.

'I challenged the Forest,' the Crone repeats, slower now, emphasising each word.

'When?'

The Crone shakes her head. She doesn't actually know, and it isn't important. 'Years ago. And I failed. The Forest took... so much from me.'

A little, hate-filled smile ripples up onto Dagne's face. She's so young, the Crone might cry.

'Liar,' Dagne says, lip curled. 'You're a pathetic, mad old hag.'

The Crone realises too late that Dagne sees herself in the Crone. That's why Dagne is so spiteful. That's why Dagne loathes her.

'No one will remember you,' the Crone says truthfully.

'I will have a place in the hero stories,' says Dagne.

The Crone shakes her head sadly. 'They will remember Elke. She's the hero of the stories that will come. But you fail, Dagne. And everyone else will forget you. The Forest will make sure of that.'

'How can you possibly know what's to become of me?' asks Dagne.

The Crone pauses. This is her last chance. She tries. 'I am what you become, Dagne. No one, not even our father, remembers us. We want change but the Forest uses that. It takes everything. You won't even have your name.'

But all this is too much and too late. Dagne spits on the ground between them and hurries to catch up to Elke and the Journeyers.

Perhaps the Crone's failure is fated. She doesn't remember meeting herself in her past, but this isn't surprising. The Forest eats the memories associated with failure. She'll never know if she's living some tortuous loop the Forest created. Nevertheless, she knows she's tied to the Forest, in the future, and here, in the past.

The Crone follows the Journeyers a while, a forgotten shadow to their adventure. She watches Elke lead her younger self through the beautiful fountaingrass clearing. The girls laugh and joke and have no care for the coming destruction.

Only the Crone remembers how that feels, to walk the chasm-edge of a grand adventure. Only the Crone remembers what will happen next.

The Crone sighs as the Journeyers cross the River and venture through the tree line. She watches until the Forest gobbles Dagne up.

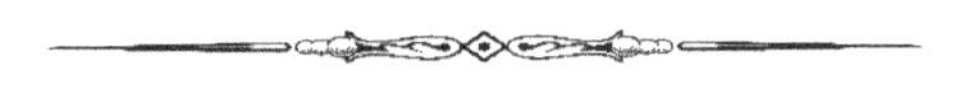

Tee Linden is a writer living south of Sydney. She's won the Sutherland Shire Resident's Prize for fiction, has been longlisted for Hachette's Richell Prize, and her work appears in anthologies from PS Publishing, Deadset Press, Margaret River Press among others.

They Stopped the Rain
Jenna Glover

The aliens came on a rainy afternoon.

I sat in front of my tent flap, cold and broke from an unsuccessful morning stint by the freeway onramp, and watched their ship part the clouds. Behind me, I could hear cars skidding to a halt, and people started to filter onto the sidewalk, necks craning, hands pointing.

It was the End Times, they shouted. We were all going to die.

Maybe that was true, I thought as the ship above me lit up something fierce.

But when the aliens came, they stopped the rain, and that was all right with me.

Jenna Glover is a science fiction and fantasy author of short fiction. Her work has appeared most recently in Martian Magazine, Haven Spec Magazine, and Flash Point SF. When she's not writing or reading, she enjoys haunting her local library, trying new recipes, playing video games, and crafting. You can read her work and learn more about her at www.jennaglover.com or follow her on Twitter and Instagram @JennaCGlover.

Family Tree
Dawn Vogel

The year my father went missing, Uncle John planted an acorn behind the house and told me we could pray at the tree that grew from it for his safe return. Uncle John and his wife, Aunt Anna, had come to take care of me at the house my father had built, since now both my parents were gone, and they didn't want to move me away from the only home I'd ever known.

The tree didn't grow well at first--it was just a stunted little thing--and neither Uncle John nor Aunt Anna seemed to pay it much mind. I, however, took a strong interest in the tree. I tied my prayers to the branches in the form of little notes, in the hopes the wind might carry my messages to my father, who, after all, was only missing.

At least that's what I believed then.

By the time three summers had passed, Uncle John began to talk about finding me a husband. He said we'd need to find a man who was more interested in a wife than her dowry. Uncle John had sold off most of my father's possessions by then to buy food and keep his supply of mead ever flowing.

I told Uncle John we should await my father's return, as he would want to ensure that whatever match was made for me was a good one. Perhaps in his absence, he'd earned me a dowry.

It took two bottles of mead before Uncle John's secret spilled.

"Your father's dead. He's not coming back."

I blinked tears from my eyes. "How do you know?"

He said nothing, but he cast his gaze toward the still small tree, barely my height, behind the house.

He didn't need to say anything. He'd planted the tree as my father's grave because he already knew my father was dead.

I fled the house.

I didn't go far, though. Just to the tree. Remnants of my messages still fluttered from the branches. The grass beneath it had grown thick and lush this year, and the leaves were thicker than they'd been in previous years, too. From an acorn, it should have been an oak, but it grew more like a pendula beech, with the branches draping downward and creating a little cave.

I wrapped my arms around the trunk and held it as though it was my father, weeping until my eyes ached, telling him how much I missed him, until I feel asleep.

When I woke the next morning, it seemed the grass had grown thicker, feeling softer than a mattress beneath me. The leaves, too, blocked out the light and sound from beyond their shield. A basket, bearing fruit and nuts, rested beside my head. I didn't recognize the basket as one of Aunt Anna's, even though I suspected she had found me while I slept and made sure I would have food when I awoke without having to face Uncle John's wrath.

His voice pierced the shelter of the tree. "That's right, Sigrid must have run away."

Other voices murmured, but none loud enough for me to hear.

"Yes, of course, we should look for her. Perhaps after our workday ends."

The other voices made a few more sounds, but then drifted away, though I heard one more thing out of Uncle John's mouth. "Good riddance to her."

I could tell he was speaking to Aunt Anna, though I didn't hear her response.

I ate the fruit and nuts, listening for the sound of Uncle John leaving to walk to the fields where he worked. Once he had been gone for what I thought was a suitable amount of time, I walked back to the house.

The door was barred. Aunt Anna never barred the door when she and I were home by ourselves, and the door could not be barred from the outside.

I knocked, hammering my fists against the door and its frame to no avail. Either she had become deaf, or she was ignoring me.

Or she couldn't hear me for some other reason.

I went to the back of the house. It wasn't cold enough yet that the windows were boarded shut. One of the window openings was large enough for me to fit through, and I pulled myself up and into the house.

Aunt Anna was in her rocking chair, working on her knitting, as though she hadn't heard me struggling to pull myself through the window.

Her darning egg sat on the table across the room. On a whim, I picked it up and dropped it on the table.

It thumped, but she didn't look up.

I carried the darning egg to where she sat.

She still didn't look up, even as I stood beside her.

I placed the darning egg in her lap, sure she would notice when something of that size and shape appeared.

But the egg rolled down her lap as she rocked, landing in her knitting basket.

Now I was baffled. I pinched myself and yelped; it didn't seem I was dreaming, nor a ghost.

Aunt Anna didn't react to my yelping, either.

Somehow, I was invisible and inaudible to her.

This warranted further testing.

I slipped back through the window after collecting a few of my things, which I stowed amongst the branches of my father's tree. Then I sat on the front steps of the house, awaiting any passers-by.

I had been unable to gain the attention of anyone passing our house all day. When I spotted Uncle John returning, I rose, ready to confront him.

Though I stood in the middle of the path to the front door, he, too, seemed oblivious to my presence. He meandered toward some wildflowers growing near the house and plucked a few stems, then passed by me without a glance.

Aunt Anna answered his knocking at the door, taking his offered flowers and smiling as she smelled them.

"No sign of Sigrid?" he asked.

"None. Should we be worried?" Aunt Anna asked.

"No. She's probably run off, thinking that will get her out of a marriage. She'll come back once she realizes she's got nowhere else to go, and she's cold and hungry." He paused and looked beyond me. "Or she'll get herself killed, like her damn-fool father."

I rushed between Aunt Anna and Uncle John, hoping by interposing myself in their midst that they might notice me. But it was still to no avail. They went about their business as if I was no longer part of their lives.

When they sat down to dinner, I snatched bits of food from their plates. Even that didn't draw their attention, even as I took enough to satiate my hunger. It assured me I wouldn't starve.

"The oddest thing happened today," Aunt Anna said, in the way of making dinner conversation with Uncle John. "I thought I'd lost my darning egg, but it turned up in the bottom of my knitting basket."

Uncle John chuckled. "You'd just as soon lose your head if it wasn't attached, my love."

"As you say. But it was peculiar."

As I listened to them, I reckoned nothing needed to change. I could still sleep in my bed and take my meals with them, and they'd be none the wiser.

But I didn't want to stay. Uncle John made it clear he didn't want me here any longer. Aunt Anna hadn't been concerned about my absence all day. They wouldn't miss me if I did run away.

If only that meant I didn't have to leave behind my father's tree.

The more I thought about my choices, the more I realized perhaps the solution wasn't for me to leave, but for me to make them leave.

The only question was how?

After Aunt Anna and Uncle John went to bed, I moved things around the house. I separated Uncle John's boots, leaving one near the front door and the other in the kitchen. I moved Aunt Anna's herb plants from the window and put her jars of dried herbs in their place. It was simple, mischievous fun, the sort of thing I might have done as a young child if I had wanted to tease my father.

Then I curled up beneath the covers of my own bed.

In the morning, Aunt Anna's voice woke me. "John, have you been moving things around in my kitchen?"

Uncle John stood in the main room, staring at his lone boot. "No, but something's moved one of my boots." He stormed into the room where I still lay in bed and frowned. It was clear from his gaze he still couldn't see me. "I barred the door last night."

"Who do you suppose could have moved things around, then? The Fair Folk?"

"Pshaw. No such thing," Uncle John said.

As the nights passed, I escalated my mischief. Uncle John tried to sit up and keep watch, but he fell asleep in his chair every time. He couldn't see me even if he had stayed awake, and both he and Aunt Anna remained oblivious to me moving things in their presence.

Aunt Anna was certain it was the Fair Folk, or something like them. She brought other women in the village over to help her look for clues, but they found nothing. They were kind enough to share stories with her, giving me a wealth of new ideas for my evening mischief.

It came to a head when I took advantage of a rainstorm that had left the ground muddy. I put sizeable clods in each of Uncle John's boots and tossed mud all over the washing hanging in the yard. More rain would come soon and rinse the mud from the washing, but the look on Aunt Anna's face when she saw it the next morning was worth it.

"John, we can't stay here any longer. I don't know if we've angered the Fair Folk or a ghost or some other malevolent being, but it's clear to me it wants us to go."

Uncle John shrugged. "Peter is dead, and Sigrid may as well be. Why shouldn't we stay here in their house?"

"Because every night, something is trying to ruin our things! You've barred the door, you've sat up late, you've even nailed the shutters closed. Whatever this is can't be kept out by normal means."

(I had been temporarily frustrated when Uncle John nailed the shutters closed, as it meant I wasn't free to come and go through the window. But I slipped in and out when Uncle John left in the morning or returned in the evening, or during the day when Aunt Anna didn't always keep the door barred.)

"So you'd have us abandon this house?"

"I can't fathom staying another night, John. If you wish to stay here alone, you can find me at my sister's house."

That ultimatum finally got through Uncle John's skull. Without Aunt Anna here, he'd have nothing to eat, no clean or mended clothes. "Alright, we'll see about finding somewhere else in the village to stay."

Aunt Anna shook her head. "No, we'll need to cross running water to evade the notice of whatever this is that has come to run us off. We must leave the village, too."

Uncle John sighed, but again, thought better than to resist his wife's insistence. "Then I suppose you'd best pack our things while I find us somewhere to stay."

My aunt and uncle left six months ago. My father's tree and I weathered the winter together, with the old leaves falling and new leaves emerging in the spring.

No one has tried to make my house their home. Apparently, Aunt Anna's stories reached far enough that everyone thinks this house is haunted or cursed.

I don't mind, though. I like the quiet of my own house. I like being able to cook the food I like and not hear any complaints.

I might not have my mother or father, but this was their house, and it's mine, too.

Now that the ground has thawed, I'm planting an acorn near my father's tree. I might have never known my mother, but now she'll have a tree, too. I'll leave her messages, just like I did for my father, and I know she'll help protect me like he did.

Someday, when I'm old and gray, I'll take another acorn and lay down near their trees when my time has come. And then we'll all be together again, a family of trees.

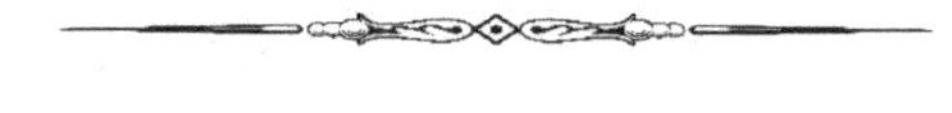

Dawn Vogel has written for children, teens, and adults, spanning genres, places, and time periods. More than 100 of her stories and poems have been published by small and large presses. Her specialties include young protagonists, siblings who bicker but love each other in the end, and things in the water that want you dead. She is a member of Broad Universe, SFWA, and Codex Writers. She lives in Seattle with her awesome husband (and fellow author), Jeremy Zimmerman, and their herd of cats. Visit her at historythatneverwas.com *or on Twitter* @historyneverwas.

Forests of Day and Night
Elana Gomel

We stopped on the way because I was getting car sick.

Jake offered me some dubious herbal remedy ("all-natural and organic"). I refused. I was mortified because normally I'm a good driver, and certainly not prone to puking on the side of the highway. But this one-lane road was crawling through the woods like a drunken snake, all sharp switchbacks and strange dips and hollows.

Leaning against Jake's Toyota, I looked at my phone to figure out where we were and was rewarded with zero signal. Even though I had been around the Bay Area for most of my life, it was still amazing to me how this world's capital of hi-tech had so many blank spots where your phone was just an expensive piece of junk. I swiped to Photos to see the picture of the house we were going to, which Jake had sent me earlier. It was a pink Mediterranean-style villa, sticking out like a sore thumb against the background of towering redwoods.

"Are you sure it's here?" I asked. People who had expensive houses in the wilderness of the Santa Cruz Mountains had more money than taste, but I still could not believe somebody would build this faux Cote d'Azur mansion in the middle of the giant forest. It was as incongruous as a seashell growing out of moss.

"I know my way."

Jake and I were not together anymore, and I was not even sure that what we used to have qualified as "together". But we were still friends. And when he texted me an invitation to come with him to this housewarming party for his Silicon Valley friends, I immediately agreed. It was not like I had anything better to do. My internship was over; my last serious relationship a distant memory; and my parents were finally divorcing after years of bickering and barely disguised hostility. My life was in bits and pieces that refused to coalesce into the tidy pattern I was sure God had in mind for me. My father was a Southern Baptist, and though I did not go to church every week anymore, I still retained his faith in the hidden order of the universe.

"Let's go," I said.

The splintered tarmac was stippled with furry shadows as the lacy tree crowns swayed high above our heads. The trees crowded the road. Their trunks were thick and gnarled, fissured with deep cracks and bulging with unsightly protrusions that looked like grinning obese faces. The bark was too red, almost scarlet.

Why would anybody want to live in a place like this?

Ours was the only car on the narrow road, which was fortunate, as there were no obvious places to pull over. On one side yawned a sharp drop, the slope overgrown with lusher vegetation than you'd expect in see in California's arid climate. On the other side, a dense grove of not-quite-redwoods clung to a precipitous rise.

"How far?" I asked Jake.

"Not far."

I realized I didn't even know the names of the couple who owned the house. I stared at the green and red chaos, feeling pieces of myself slough off and fall by the wayside. The trees grew larger and larger, towering above us and piercing the pale sky. Redwoods, the pride of California, had always existed on the margins of my perception, an eco-friendly addendum to the real world of offices, highways, malls, and overpriced rentals. Now they were swallowing me up.

"How is Rishma?" I asked Jake. Rishma was his current girlfriend, a tiny programmer with larger-than-life ambitions.

"We broke up," Jake said.

I was astonished. I liked Risma; she seemed to be a far better fit for Jake with his high-tech background than myself. She liked me too. When I told her I was thinking of changing my name, she was supportive – as opposed to Jake who insisted on calling me by the name I no longer felt was mine.

I opened my mouth to ask for details when a movement outside drew my attention.

Something hopped from one low-hanging branch to another. A squirrel? But no, it was much bigger than your average pest and moved much slower, with an almost liquid awkwardness, as if a clump of some sticky substance dripped down. Jake speeded up, and though I craned my head to look back, I was left with an incongruous image of a large ball of dough hanging from the tree.

The trees reached across the narrow road, and now I was sure they were not redwoods anymore, but my scant botanical knowledge had no name for them. Some of them were freakishly tall; some squat and misshapen. Their scarlet trunks leered with gaping mouths: a living imitation of the Scream. Their naked boughs were too low to the ground, burdened with long skinny clumps of twigs like skeletal fingers. We rounded a corner where the slope to the side disappeared. The trees were so close together that both sides of the road were plunged into crawling darkness. The shadows squirmed on the acid green of fat moss cushions that covered the ground. I could not see the sun anymore; and the light was failing, getting brownish like weak tea, even though it was still hours till sunset.

"Jake…" I whispered. He looked at me with the empty dark holes of his eyes.

It was all wrong, of course.

I had a perfect memory of that weekend, ten years ago. It was only natural that I did. You don't forget the day you meet your future husband. I was remembering that day as I went about my usual boring routine. We were working from home, and every moment of solitude was precious. So, when Rita finally dozed off, and Michael went into his office, I sat at the kitchen counter with my tablet, scrolling through the ten-year-old album titled simply "That June". Here it was: the selfie with a giant pseudo-Mediterranean villa in the background, surrounded by manzanitas and redwoods. There were people milling around, but the picture was out of focus, and the ambient lights scattered around the yard dissolved into jellyfish-like blobs, encroaching upon the dim silhouettes of the guests. Michael must have been one of these shadows, but it was early in the evening, and it was only later when, tired and drunk, I stepped out onto the giant deck incongruously decorated with cast-iron statues that I saw him there. He did not try to chat me up. We just stood together in silence, watching the stars pop up in the glassy sky, undimmed by light pollution from the Bay. Then he turned to me and smiled…and the rest, as they say, is history.

But what history?

I fiddled with the selfie but the more I expanded it, the more the entire thing broke down into a sticky mélange of indistinct blobs and furry shadows. The pink wall of the villa grew into a fleshy flank studded with protuberances like a sow's tits. The guests in the background became looming ghosts trailing ragged smears of clothing. My own face metamorphosed into an unsightly collection of makeup blobs and untrimmed eyebrows. But here it was, just on the edge of the picture and totally out of focus: a mop of dark hair and a sliver of greasy forehead.

Jake!

I had never known anybody named Jake.

Or had I? My memory was strangely bifurcated. The name wriggled on the edges of my awareness like an annoying insect – like a large centipede whose multiple hairy legs tickled my brain. This image was so specific and so weird that I grabbed my forehead as if trying to squeeze it out. And that was when I saw it. Among the thumbnail images on my iPad, there was a tiny square with something black and hairy against the poisonous green background. I clicked on it – and saw a picture of Michael and myself holding hands. Back to the thumbnail display – and among the familiar photos of our first dates, there were tiny and ominous intrusions. A mouth opened in a scream but with yellow pseudopods emerging from between its teeth. A single eye dangling from a glossy green leaf. The heaving surface of a bloated stomach; a blob of dissolving flesh. But when I clicked on each of them, they became familiar and comforting images of our courtship.

I heard Rita over the baby monitor and rushed in to settle her. Her sleep-warmed body nestled in my arms, so perfect and so unarguably real. When I had been pregnant with her, I had been obsessed by fear of something going wrong. I could never get enough sonograms and expert opinions. I had had nightmares of the swirling organic goo in my womb solidifying into uncouth shapes; of the fetus developing extra arms and legs or missing the brain.

Nothing like this had happened. My 10-month-old daughter was perfect. My marriage was perfect. My life was just what it was meant to be.

And I had never known anybody named Jake.

As Rita drifted back into sleep, I stepped out onto the deck. It was funny how Michael and I eventually settled into life in the redwoods, even though I had always considered myself a city girl. My mother was from London originally and had now gone back to live in Brixton. I had spent my childhood in San Carlos – not a metropolis but not the boondocks either. But here we were, in our large solitary home surrounded by the whisper of endless trees, with our nearest neighbors half a mile away and with daily visits from wild turkeys and deer. And I was happy.

Wasn't I?

Michael came out on the deck with a large glass of Pinot Grigio which he silently handed to me. I leaned into him, watching swift shadows of bats streak against the fading purple of twilight. There were more of them than usual.

"Are you done?" I asked. Michael worked for a medical-device startup, writing their software.

"For now," he said.

One of the bats almost strafed my head, and I heard a high-pitched shriek reverberating in my bones. It passed by too quickly but there was something wrong with it. Did it have three wings, the third flapping on its back like an ungainly sail? No, of course not. The darkness smudged everything into the sea of inchoate forms and unfinished movements. There were no streetlights, and the dim glow from the living room failed to pierce the darkness.

"Michael," I asked, "do you remember how we met?"

I could not see his face, but I knew he smiled.

"Marital quiz time? Of course, I do. You were standing on the deck, alone, and I came out because I had been watching you all evening, trying to screw up my courage to talk to you."

That was not what I remembered; Michael had already been on the deck when I came out. But fine, if he wanted to weave a more romantic narrative. I knew how unreliable and pliant memory was. We are all making up stories in our head, imposing order on the chaos of existence.

"Did you know the hosts? What were their names?"

He shrugged and, and it was as if the dark shrugged with him.

"Have no idea. I came with a friend."

"What friend?"

"Erin."

I drained the wineglass in a single gulp.

"Did I ever meet her?" I asked, trying to keep my voice steady.

"I don't think so. But she was a friend, not a girlfriend. Well, sort of."

He went back inside to finish whatever piece of software he had been coding, and I stayed in the dark, clutching the smoothness of the wineglass as if it were my only defense against the shadowy chaos of the forest.

I never used this name anymore. After my mother had left, I was so angry with her that I refused to go by the name she had chosen for me, adopting instead my middle name, my father's Biblical choice: Sara.

I was Sara now, and that was how I had introduced myself to Michael on our first date.

Hadn't I?

I drove up the narrow winding road, Rita strapped into the baby seat behind me. It was hard to find the time to do it. Working from home was supposed to be about time management and flexibility. For me, it had become a quicksand, sucking me in as I struggled to keep my head above the advancing tide of Google meets, and shared calendars, and accumulating emails. Rita's naps and playtimes doled out precious moments of freedom, but then there was Michael. Even when he was in the office, I did not feel alone. His presence permeated the house: both a defense against the solitude of the redwoods and a subtle taint like the premonition of a migraine. When he had to go to the office in Menlo Park, he spent five minutes apologizing for leaving "his girls" alone

And now here I was. Driving into the woods to look for a pink Mediterranean-style villa.

After our conversation, I drank a second glass of wine and sat in the living room with my iPad, going through the Google photos of ten years ago. Michael eventually went to bed, leaving me with the whispering darkness beyond our house's insubstantial walls and the memories that ran and dripped like a poorly made watercolor.

I had two distinct stories of that evening. In one, I drove to the villa invited by some girlfriend whose name I could not recall. I was bored. I went out onto the deck to watch the somber forest sunset and met a guy who had already been there. My future husband.

In the second memory, I drove to the villa with a friend with benefits named Jake, and something bad happened on the way. Something so bad that the memory was cut short and left dangling like a piece of ripped-off cloth.

The thing was, I knew Jake; I could visualize his shock of wiry hair and his annoying habit of ending every sentence with "like". I knew that after we split up, he had a girlfriend named Rishma. I knew I had met her and loved the henna drawing she had on her hand. And at the same time, I could not connect either Jake or Rishma to anything else in my life. I leafed through my memories, the pages in the storybook that was myself. My suburban home; my parents perpetually sniping at each other; my high school where I was neither on top nor on the bottom of the social pole; University of San Francisco with my bland major in Business Administration; my boyfriends; my travels; my marriage; Rita's birth…Nowhere was there a blank spot where the face of Jake could possibly be inserted. And yet, there it was, floating in my mind like a pricked balloon, distorted into a softly drooping shape.

And what was that about Michael's friend-cum-girlfriend with my discarded name? He knew my full name, of course; it was on our marriage certificate, but he also knew I never used "Erin" anymore. Had he been making fun of me? Had there been a disguised hostility in his voice? I loved my husband but there is a dark penumbra surrounding each one of us to which nobody has access. Not even ourselves.

Or was it just a coincidence? Certainly, Erin is far from an uncommon name.

Just like those phantom thumbnails in my photo albums, random memories of Jake kept popping up and disappearing. And they were somehow mixed with images of distorted trees, and dripping hunks of flesh, and skittering animals in the scant undergrowth that looked like no animals at all.

A movement on the narrow road ahead made me stomp on the brakes. With an ear-piercing screech, the car went sliding of the road until it miraculously stabilized. The nose of my Tesla hung over the slope overgrown with bulbous red bushes. Something snapped under the wheel with an obscenely liquid gulp. Rita woke up and wailed. Whatever it was I almost hit was nowhere to be seen.

I hushed her and sat with my eyes closed for a moment, trying to get my breathing under control. I had never hit a deer on the road, but I knew it could happen. The animals, stupid and unculled by hunters, had lost all caution. Fortunately, they were also skittish and would run away when spooked.

I opened my eyes and realized that my almost-roadkill had come back. And also, that it was not a deer.

Sitting in the middle of the narrow, splintered tarmac was something that looked like a giant owl. I knew there were big owls elsewhere in the arboreal forests of the North, but this one was easily as tall as myself. Pale and fat and dripping, it stared at me with round cataract-covered eyes.

Dripping?

The owl was not covered with feathers but with sticky webs, woven together into a gluey coat that imitated feathers, much like plastic can imitate fur. Pieces of it plopped onto the tarmac. Its eyes were fogged yellowish disks. The only hard part was the cruel curving beak, sticking out of the heaving muck.

It stumbled toward the car. I screamed and hit the accelerator.

There was a gooey explosion, and the windshield was splattered with liquid filth. I was blinded and deafened by Rita's crying. It made me come to my senses and stop. I could have easily driven off the road into the swollen scarlet bushes.

Scarlet?

The wipers failed to clean the muck off the windshield. I unbuckled, took

Rita into my arms, and stepped out of the car.

My golden Tesla was covered in sticky webs, as if an enormous spider had been at work. Something bony and curved lay on the hood. A sick stench tickled my sinuses.

The trees overhanging the road were distended and deformed, their trunks the color of drying blood, their foliage burnt-black. The slope that ran down off the road on the left side was overgrown with what looked like corals, their colors as bright and unreal as an acid dream.

I looked at my daughter. Rita's eyes were wide open, taking it all in. Her soft mouth split in a toothless grin, and she babbled, pointing to the poisonous kaleidoscope of vegetation. She had already started saying "mama" and "dada" but the sounds coming from her now were in no language I knew.

A movement behind me made me look back. The sticky webs draping the car were crawling, slithering all over the bodywork. They fell onto the ground in folds of mucous matter and quickly reconstituted themselves into the owl. From close up, I could see that it was no more than a crude approximation of a bird, like a statue made of slime. One shapeless wing reached out, lengthening as it did so, and picked up the beak off the hood, putting it into the middle of the drooping face. Two dim eyes blinked open, one below the other.

I turned around and ran up the road, despite Rita's protesting gurgle.

I rounded the bend, and here it was: a pink pseudo-Mediterranean villa, surrounded by crouching trees that were like no trees on Earth. Its windows shimmered in oily colors.

I looked back. The owl was dragging itself wetly behind us.

I walked to the door that was open and stepped inside.

The detritus of the party was still scattered in the living space: used paper plates, and empty bottles, and dirty serving dishes. The couches held imprints of sprawling bodies, and when I touched one, it was warm. But there was nobody around. The house was empty.

Except when I walked through the open-plan living room and stepped onto the deck. And here he was, his untidy hair sticking out every which way, his toothy grin welcoming me and my daughter.

"Hello, Jake," I said.

He tried to give us a hug, but I backed off, even though Rita squirmed and reached toward him.

"What's going on?" I asked.

"I tried to do the right thing. But you had to come back. Well, I'm kind of glad you have. It's lonely here on my own."

"Where is 'here'?"

"Where we have always been. The forest of the night."

"What does it even mean?"

"Your father told you, didn't he? God creates order out of chaos, time out of randomness. But there are always leftovers. Unused lives, untidy, random, bent out of shape. Things that don't fit. For every forest of day there is a forest of night where things grow like fungi on a rotten tree, with no rhyme or reason."

"That's not in any Bible lesson I got."

"But you lost your faith anyway when your mother died."

"My mother is not dead! She lives in Brixton!"

But even as I was saying it, a different knowledge was forming in my head, a different story: my mother's glassy eyes as she lay in the hospital bed, surrounded by beeping hardware…

"Leftovers. Things that could have happened but did not. Thrown into the dark, to rot, and grow, and breed. I tried to steer you toward the forest of the day. To give you the life you wanted. But God had other plans, or maybe, no plan at all."

"This is bullshit!" I screamed. "I should have never come back!"

"You have never left."

"It was ten years ago, Jake. I have a husband and a daughter."

"This is one story. One that could have happened but did not."

"Why not?"

"Because I killed you, Erin."

The owl followed me as I went back to the car. I tried to imagine what creature had been shaped out of primordial chaos to leave behind this ungainly leftover. Not that it mattered. I was not afraid of it anymore. The dead are fearless.

As Jake explained it, he had been so upset by the breakup with Rishma that he had decided to kill himself. But he did not want to go alone into the forest of the night. So, he took me with him.

Rita was crawling on the carpet, as I rooted in the baby-bag for her snack. Jake was making silly faces at my daughter. At my daughter who did not exist.

"I don't believe you," I said. "I am alive. My daughter is alive. You are just a phantom of the past. You cannot hurt us."

"I never wanted to hurt you, Erin." Jake said. "I'm sorry."

"Sorry does not cut it," I said and marched out of the pink villa, littered with the remnants of the party that ended ten years ago. The deformed trees whispered behind my back.

As I drove back, I was trying to come to terms with what Jake had told me. According to him, he had strangled me and hanged himself in the redwoods ten years ago. But somehow, because it had been such a random, chaotic, unpredictable crime, time had bifurcated at that moment. I could have easily escaped. He could have changed his mind. So, there were two of me now. Sara, living in the forest of the day with her husband and daughter, following God's orderly plan for her. And Erin, dead and buried in the forest of the night.

But wasn't God supposed to be everywhere?

In my father's Bible, God created the world out of chaos. But didn't it mean that chaos preceded the creation, and was still there, crawling just beyond the order of the universe, inexhaustible, patient, and omnipresent. The forest of the day growing out of the eternal darkness of the forest of the night, always ready to collapse back into it.

But it did not matter. I was alive. I had escaped.

As I drove, the forest of monstrous shapes slowly gave way to the familiar redwoods. Even my cellphone blinked on, catching the dregs of a signal. But I did not need it. I knew where I was. My home was close.

I parked and walked to the door, seeing Michael's car in the driveway. He was puttering in the kitchen.

"Home so soon?" I asked. "Weren't you supposed to be at work the whole day?"

"Time is flexible," he said, hunched over the stove, getting Rita's bottle ready.

I sat her in the highchair. Her head was drooping; she must be tired. Her onesie was smeared with some sticky goo. I brushed the velvety fabric, trying to get the stickiness off. Why did babies always get muck all over themselves? It is as if their bodies leave behind drippy residue as they are being formed into their proper shapes. Leftovers of growth.

The stickiness would not go away, no matter how I rubbed it off. A drip of mucus fell onto the tray.

"You shouldn't take Rishma with you when you go for a drive," Michael said. "It's dangerous."

"Rishma? Our daughter's name is Rita."

"What's in a couple of letters, Erin? These are just leftovers."

"You never call me Erin," I said, refusing to look outside where scarlet shadows were creeping over the redwoods.

"It's your name. And you never call me by my middle name either."

"Michael Jacob Greenhouse," I said. "Jake."

My husband turned around and looked at me with the empty dark holes of his eyes.

Elana Gomel is an academic and an award-winning writer. Born in Ukraine, she has lived and taught in many countries, including the US, Israel, Italy, and Hong Kong. She is the author of six non-fiction books and numerous articles on subjects such as narrative theory, posthumanism, science fiction, and serial killers. As a fiction writer, she has published more than a hundred fantasy and science fiction stories, several novellas, and five novels. She is a member of HWA and can be found at

https://www.citiesoflightanddarkness.com/ and on social media

Suspended Sentence
Maureen Bowden

The newspaper headline said, "Woman fakes death to avoid paying window cleaner." Charlotte Cresswell could almost hear the readers laughing, just as the court had laughed when her barrister entered a guilty plea to the charges of wasting police time and theft of £20 intended for the window cleaner. He asked for mitigation due to diminished responsibility. She believed she was the victim of a curse. Obviously seriously deluded.

The judge wasn't laughing. "Miss Cresswell," he said. "Have you any idea how many thousands of pounds of public money were spent dredging the River Mersey searching for your body after you expressed your intention to jump off the New Brighton ferry?"

She hung her head. "No, Your Honour. I didn't think anyone would bother looking."

"I sentence you to six months in prison, suspended for two years. You will attend monthly consultations with a psychologist appointed by the court, and you have to pay the window cleaner."

Six months was nothing. She'd been living under a suspended sentence for ten years. Lying on the shrink's couch she cast her mind back and told him the story.

She was fourteen years old, hanging out with the cool kids during the summer holidays. A few feet along the pavement a window cleaner was perched on a ladder. His bucket was balanced on the bedroom window sill and he was warbling Adele's 'Someone Like You' while he cleaned the windows.

Jordan Sampson, the nerd of the pack, stepped into the road. "It's bad luck to walk under a ladder," he said.

Charlotte sniggered, "don't be stupid," and tempting fate she sashayed along the pavement, and with the ladder overhead she looked up and waved at the window cleaner. The bucket wobbled, slipped off the sill and bashed her on the head.

The next thing she remembered was Death reaching out his hand and helping her to her feet. He wasn't a scary skeleton in a hooded cloak. He was a friendly-looking old gentleman wearing black leather trousers and a tee-shirt with 'Elvis Lives' printed on the front. Charlotte glanced down at her inert body lying on the ground. Her voice trembled. "What happened?"

"You walked under a ladder, my dear, and every action has a consequence. In this case the consequence is me, namely Death."

She started to cry. "But I'm only fourteen. It's not fair."

He nodded. "I agree, it's a little harsh, so here's what I suggest. You won't die before you pay the window cleaner. Agreed?"

"Agreed." It was a straw to clutch.

She woke up with a sore head. The cool kids were milling around her, the window cleaner was cursing teenage morons, and Jordan Sampson, while looking smug, was lecturing, "I told you so."

Charlotte reached her early twenties living with her widowed mother, and reluctant to find accommodation of her own in case it involved dirty windows. She helped with all other household expenses but her mother paid the window cleaner.

One summer afternoon, during her annual leave from Giovanni's Pizza Parlour, she was having a duvet day watching daytime TV. Her mother was meeting an old friend in town, for coffee and a catch-up.

During the hundredth repeat of an episode of 'Midsomer Murders', Charlotte's phone rang. Her mother's voice said, "Charlotte, I forgot to tell you. The window cleaner's calling for his money this afternoon. It's in an envelope behind the clock. Will you pay him, please? See you later. 'Bye." She ended the call.

Charlotte panicked. She had to get away before the window cleaner showed up. The weight of her predicament finally overwhelmed her. How could she live with this curse any longer? Somewhere there must be a sanctuary where window cleaners could be permanently avoided, and nobody would find her and bring her back. She dressed, turned off the TV and wrote a note to her mother. "Dear Mum, I'm tired of my life and of being a burden to you. I'm going to catch the New Brighton Ferry and when it reaches the middle of the river I'll jump off. I love you. Charlotte."

She didn't mean it, of course. Once she was somewhere safe she'd write to her mother and apologise for worrying her. Now what? She needed money and didn't have any. The envelope behind the clock contained a twenty-pound note. She pocketed it and left the house.

A plan was forming in her mind. A New-Age Travellers' commune was currently squatting in Princes Park. The only windows the travellers possessed were in their campers and trucks and it was unlikely that they'd hire anyone to clean them.

Reaching the park she approached a bearded man with waist-length braids, and a woman with no braids but blue spikes. Braids said, "You look lost."

"Story of my life." Charlotte said. "Can I join you? I'll work for my keep. All I need is somewhere to sleep and enough to eat. I can give you £20. It's all I have."

Spikes said, "Why do want to join us?"

"I'm running away."

"From what?"

"A curse."

Braids said, "Fair enough. What do we call you?"

She thought quickly, and remembered her favourite doll from years before the unfortunate episode with the ladder, "Call me Rose."

Spikes said, "Rose what?"

"Rose Budd."

Braids said, "Okay Rosebud, you're in."

During the next few weeks she worked harder than she had in her life, cooking, washing, feeding dogs and changing babies' nappies. She didn't mind. She felt safe.

Then it all went wrong. One of the travellers was an undercover police officer sniffing out illegal activity: any illegal activity. It didn't matter what. His best friend in the Force was directing the dredging operation searching for Charlotte's body. They discussed the case over a beer in the 'Dagger and Duck'. Friend showed Undercover the missing girl's photo. It was a fair cop.

The shrink said, "Let us assume for the present that your encounter with Death actually took place, Charlotte. I want you to consider that you have misinterpreted the curse."

"Nice try, Doc," she said, "but I know what I heard."

"Quite. You heard that you won't die before you pay the window cleaner, but you don't know how long you'll live after you pay him. It could be another sixty years. The actual curse is that if you never pay the window cleaner you'll never die."

She sat up and stared at him. "I'll live forever?"

"It's up to you, but I certainly wouldn't want to live forever. That's a humdinger of a curse."

She frowned, then gasped, then howled with laughter. "I got it back to front. I've been so stupid. What do I do now?"

"Come and see me again next month but in the meantime I suggest you pay the window cleaner."

"I can't. I gave the £20 to the travellers. I don't have any money."

"You do. You'll receive sickness benefit until I decide that your responsibility is sufficiently undiminished for you to return to work."

She skipped home, laughing all the way, and hugged her mother. "I'm okay, Mum. You don't have to worry about me anymore. Get a life of your own. Marry the old friend you keep meeting for coffee."

Her mother blushed. "How did you know about…?"

"I'm not a complete idiot, just an incomplete one. Where does our window cleaner live?"

"Number 42 Jubilee Drive, Why?"

"Lend me £20. I want to pay him."

Her mother shook her head. "There's no need. He knows I only have my widow's pension so he let me off with it."

"You won't be paying. I'll give it back to you when I get my sickness benefit. I have to do this, trust me."

"Okay, but don't pull another stunt like the last one or I won't invite you to the wedding."

She ran all the way to Jubilee Drive and knocked at the window cleaner's door. He answered it. She said, "Hello, I'm Mrs Cresswell's daughter and I owe you this. Sorry I took so long." She handed him the £20 note.

"Thank you, Miss. I'm glad you're not dead."

She turned, smiling, and walked away, feeling the weight of the curse lift from her shoulders. Skipping along the pavement in a state of euphoria she failed to see the ladder in front of her. She failed to see Jordan Sampson at the top of it. She failed to see the heavy tin of wood preservative balanced on the windowsill while Jordan dipped his brush in the contents and applied it to the window frame. She was under the ladder when the tin slipped, dropped, and cracked her skull.

Death reached out his hand and helped her to her feet.

Maureen Bowden is a Liverpudlian, living with her musician husband in North Wales. She has had 172 stories and poems accepted by paying markets. She was nominated for the 2015 international Pushcart Prize, and in 2019 Hiraeth Books published an anthology of her stories, 'Whispers of Magic.' She also writes song lyrics, mostly comic political satire, set to traditional melodies. Her husband has performed them in folk music clubs throughout the UK. She loves her family and friends, rock 'n' roll, Shakespeare, and cats.

Gardens, Ghosts and War
H.L. Fullerton

When Harold was four, he found a sword in the garden. It was encrusted with dirt, having been unearthed from the spot where Mother wanted the gardener to plant tulips, and long as he was tall. Nanny wanted to take it away from him, but Mother said let him play. Harold used both hands to lever the sword into the air in front of him and promptly began marching toward the stone wall that demarked their grass, trees, and flowers from everyone else's.

Nanny tried to coax him back to the great lawn, but Harold ignored her the way he'd seen Mother do when someone wasn't important. "He'll hurt himself, climbing that wall," Nanny called and Mother rose from her bench and strolled over to her son. Mother had a strict 'hands off' policy when it came to Nanny and Harold, and while Nanny might be tempted to pinch Harold in the nursery, she didn't dare haul him back to the safety of the garden with her employer looking on.

Harold was at the foot of the wall, which came up to mid-chest on him, and had rested the point of the sword on a jutting rock.

"That's a nice sword you have there, Harold," Mother said. Mother was much taller than the wall and could easily lift Harold and the sword over it. But Harold was going to conquer the wall himself--without Mother's help.

"I found it in the garden." Harold moved the sword's blade from facing front to rear echelon. He'd never seen a man drag a sword, but Harold couldn't figure a better way of climbing with it. He placed one small foot on the rock where the sword had rested and gripped another higher rock with his chubby fingers.

"Where are you headed, honey?"

"I'm going to war," Harold said, all his concentration on the stones before him.

"Oh," Mother said. "Without your shield?"

Harold stopped climbing and looked up at her. "I don't have a shield."

"Every soldier needs a shield," Mother said, plucking Harold from his perch and depositing him on the ground, facing the house.

"Do you think there's one buried in the garden?"

"We can look," Mother said. "And if there's not, I'll make you one for your birthday."

So Harold dragged his sword back to the garden and Mother gave him a spade and he dug and dug and dug, but he never found a shield. The gardener though had plenty of freshly turned dirt for tulip bulbs.

Harold was four and three-quarters when he first saw the ghost. Only, Harold didn't realize the soldier rooting in the garden was a ghost. He thought it a neighbor trying to steal Mother's tulips. He ran inside to get his sword, but when he returned--followed closely by Nanny who had misplaced him but for a second--the scoundrel was gone.

When Harold turned five, his mother gave him a shield made from a silver plate the servants had dropped one too many times and leather straps confiscated from an old saddle. He slipped it onto his left arm and awkwardly lifted his sword, now free from dirt, with both hands. The sword wasn't too heavy for him, but its length

and his height made balancing it a trick. He could manage, but it meant his new shield was useless to prevent an attack.

Before the cake was served, Harold headed for the front door.

"Harold," Mother called. "Where are you going? There's cake. And ice cream."

"I have my shield. I have my sword. I'm going to war."

"But, Harold, what about the lessons?"

"I don't like Nanny's lessons."

"Not from Nanny. I hired a war tutor. You're very good with the sword, but I thought he could show you how to fight with sword *and* shield."

Harold stopped and thought about that. He tilted his arm and looked at his new shield. "Does he know a lot about swords?"

Mother nodded.

"And war?"

Mother nodded again.

"Can I have ice cream first?" Harold asked, climbing back into his chair and Mother said, "Of course."

His tutor told him he had to be taller to join the army. Harold was disappointed. Each day he asked, "Am I tall enough yet?" and the tutor shook his head. But Harold learned to fight--with a sword and shield and with fists and knives. Mother said he made a very good soldier.

When Harold was as tall as a Visigoth, Mother fired his instructor. She gave Harold a new sword--made just for him, a real shield with their family crest upon it, and a pair of boots. "Well, Harold," she said. "I guess it's time."

"Goodbye, Mother. I'll write."

"I'll look forward to your letters. Your father never sent any. I'm glad you decided to let Nanny teach you your letters." And maths. For a soldier had to know how to spend his pay and what a new sword should cost. Harold turned to go, his pack upon his shoulder. "Harold? Who shall you fight for?"

"The army."

"Yes, but which army? There's so many. Which one will you pick?"

And Harold knew much about fighting, but little about choosing sides. "Which do you think best, Mother?"

"Oh, I couldn't say, dear. I don't know much about armies and politics. Did your tutor mention anything?" But Tutor hadn't.

"What side did Father choose?"

"That was so many wars ago, I can hardly remember. Blue, I think. With gold buttons. Maybe bronze. But a man can hardly choose an army based upon the uniform, can he?"

Harold thought, brow furrowed. "I'll pick the side that deserves to win."

"Very good, dear. It's just...how will you know which side is superior? I've asked the gardener, over and over, whether ragged robin or nasturtiums will do best by the pond and he says either will do just fine. I think I'll have him plant both. I hope choosing an army is easier than picking flowers."

Harold couldn't fight for two armies, of that he was sure. "Maybe I should learn what each side is fighting for first."

"There are some very fine thinkers on the subject," Mother said. So she hired another tutor and Harold learned about philosophy and ethics, strategy and rhetoric. His new tutor was especially enamored of peace and lectured on the concept ad infinitum. Harold barely had time to practice his swordsmanship.

At twelve, Harold saw Iris and lost his heart. He was supposed to be writing an essay on the art of peace maintenance, but instead was running drills. Iris smiled at him and Harold dropped his sword. She giggled; called him Sir Knight--and all that fustian about chivalry started making sense.

When he turned thirteen, Harold told Mother he was going to marry Iris. Mother said, "She's sixteen, Harold. You and Iris will have to wait until you're the same age."

This seemed the same as having to be a particular height to join the army and Harold was good enough at maths to realize he could never catch up to Iris no matter how many years she waited. He asked Mother, "How old was Father when he married you?"

"Not thirteen," Mother said.

"Fine, I'll marry Iris when *I'm* sixteen, and then I'll go to war." It worried Harold that there were so many wars he'd already missed. He didn't want to miss out on Iris.

"But what will Iris do when you go?"

"She'll stay here with you, Mother. Help out." Harold thought Mother would like the company; she'd had only him since Father left and would be lonely with him gone. Mother, however, wasn't as sure. She said, "Iris has a mother, she may not want two. Or you may wish to take her with you. Some couples can't bear to be parted. Have I ever told you about Great-Grandmother's Bloody Proposal and the Treaty of Crumb?"

She had, but Harold listened anyway. He'd adored this tale as a child, and Mother never told it the same way twice; each account more frightening than the last. This version was the bloodiest yet. It made Harold forget all about Iris waiting for him in the lane.

Harold officially met the ghost when he was fourteen. He stood in Mother's garden, waiting for Iris. He heard footsteps--heavier than Iris', but mayhap she wore boots, it was a muddy day-- turned, smile at the ready, and found a soldier rummaging about the flowers, batting blooms this way and that, mumbling curses and other nonsense.

"Excuse me, sir," Harold said. "You're trampling our flowers."

Except he wasn't really. The flowers swayed as if disturbed by a slight breeze, nothing more. Harold took in the soldier's dress--mail shirt and a colorful--but empty--baldric. The man looked familiar and the hunched posture... The memory of a man lost among tulips woke in Harold's mind, vivid and bright. "You there!" Harold said, calling upon an authoritative tone borrowed from Mother (because Iris had mentioned a few times that if Harold wanted to be a soldier so badly, the first person he ought to defend was himself), "You're trespassing."

The soldier looked up; his mail clinked. He said, "The dead go where we want. Now go away, boy. I'm busy."

"It's Harold, Ghost. Not 'boy.'"

"Ghost?! I'll have you know, I'm--" The ghost paused, looked puzzled, then disappeared, like a puff of smoke up a chimney. In his wake, came Mother and her needlepoint. She asked about the whereabouts of his sword--surely, a soldier wasn't in the habit of forgetting his sword?--and rather than lie about arranging to meet Iris, Harold confessed to conversing with a ghost.

"Can't imagine what a ghost could tell you that I could not," Mother said, and Harold wondered how much the ghost remembered of armying.

Turned out, the ghost made an excellent skewering partner. His baldric and hands might be empty, but his mail chimed nicely when struck.

At sixteen, Harold proposed to Iris and invited her to follow him into battle. "Maybe," Iris said, "you should go to war first, then come back and marry me."

It made sense to Harold. He'd loved swords before he loved Iris and war always came before peace. Otherwise, one couldn't appreciate it in quite the same way, all the scholars said so. Luckily, there was a war going on and Harold had already decided which side ought to win and thus the side he should fight for. "Does that mean we can't kiss?"

"Oh, no. We can do that," Iris said. So he accepted Iris' counteroffer and told Mother his plan.

"So, Harold, whose side have you chosen? Is it one you believe in with all your heart?"

"It is." Harold wore the same expression he had at four when he tried to climb the stone wall with his newfound sword.

Mother kissed Harold's forehead. "Then you've chosen wisely. Be safe. You're the last of us. If you don't make it home...

"You know, your father left me you

before he went off. I haven't been feeling well of late and I'd dearly love some grandchildren to coddle. Do you think this Iris could be persuaded?"

Harold was torn. There was a world out there in need of saving. He'd already waited so long. He searched Mother's face for signs of illness. She looked older than he remembered--and tired. Especially when compared to Iris' flushed face. A child to carry on the family name wasn't so outlandish a request. "I'll ask," he said, blushing a little.

"That would be nice," Mother said and took to her bed.

The ghost, too, thought baby-making an excellent idea. "Make a man out of you," he told Harold, who pointed out the ghost had claimed the same thing about the army. "There are lots of ways to become a man," the ghost said. "But you'll never be one until you cut those apron strings. If you can't do it, hand me a sword and I'll do it for you."

Harold didn't think giving a bloodthirsty dead soldier a weapon was a good idea. "You've been dead so long you might mistake a neck for a string," Harold said, declining the offer.

"Trussed up like a turkey in an oven," the ghost muttered. "Bet you'd stick around to see the fool thing born."

And Harold, who'd never known his father, not for one second of his life, thought that a sensible suggestion, even if it was made in jest.

Iris circumvented the topic of babies altogether. She said, "If your mother knew how much you wanted to go to war, she wouldn't keep you here."

"She isn't. She's ill. The doctor says..."

"-...whatever your mother tells him to say."

Harold remembered the doctor quarantining him when he littler, telling him the army didn't take young men with fevers or spots. Sentiments his mother had shared before enlisting the doctor's expert opinion. Iris might have a point, but Harold wanted to be fair. He'd taken many of the philosophies pushed upon him by Tutor Two to heart, especially those on equity. "Mother has never asked me to choose between her and soldiering." He wondered if Iris would make him choose between her wishes and his mother's. Mother said she might. "Don't you want babies?"

"When you were a little boy, whose sword did you find in the garden?" Iris said, her hand resting on his. "Was it your father's?"

"Father took his sword with him when he left."

"Are you sure?" Iris said. Harold wasn't. He was repeating what Mother had told him. He thought about Father, how little he knew of the man. Three things really: Father was a soldier; Father got Mother pregnant; Father left. Oh and he had his father's eyes. So four things.

Harold always thought 'Father left' meant Father returned to warring. How Mother went on about men leaving for war, not thinking about those left at home. Yet she'd never actually said Father went off to war. That was Harold's inference. "Why does it matter?" he asked.

Iris shook her head. "Your mother should let you go." But Harold stayed and Iris ran off with some soldier she met in town.

When Harold was seventeen, the ghost told him he was a man and it was time he did man things--like kill other men. "If I had my sword, I'd show you. I had it but a moment ago."

"You've never had a sword," Harold said.

"You could lend me yours." The ghost was always asking for things: a bit of cloth, a button, a scrap of leather for his boot, a dram, a crumb of cake, a sword; and Harold always refused. Harold didn't trust the ghost. He seemed a sly sort.

"I need mine to run you through." Since Iris' desertion, Harold practiced his swordsmanship every day. Skewering a ghost was cathartic. Decapitating one was gloriously epiphanic, even if it did retain its head.

"Did I ever tell you about the time I--"

"Yes," Harold said, stabbing the ghost in his liver. The difficulty with ghosts is that they--at least this one--seemed doomed to repetition. Same stories, same actions. Same complaints. Harold worried all soldiers might be like this one--a very disappointing thought.

The ghost brushed a daffodil aside with his booted foot. Searching for his weapon.

"Eyes up, man," Harold ordered and the ghost's head snapped up. In that moment, two truths stung Harold to his quick. The ghost and he wore matching faces--*they had the same eyes*--and Mother fenced better than any opponent he'd ever encounter. Only she used words as her blade.

"Mother," Harold said when they sat down to dinner. "There is a ghost in the garden who wears my face."

"Oh?"

"It makes me wonder if there is also a dead man wearing my face buried in the garden."

"There are plenty of dead men composting the garden, Harold. Our home is no stranger to war. Have you forgotten the Treaty of Crumb? Your ancestors' blood fell like rain that day. Surely, some of them resembled you."

Harold tried the soup, but found it too coppery given the discussion. He settled for picking apart a roll. "This ghost--I've only met the one--has my eyes. I wondered if he might be my father."

Mother said, "Don't be silly, Harold. Ghosts can't have children. Tell me, is the soup too thin?"

Harold took another spoonful of soup and said, "Soup can't be thin, Mother. It's a puddle in a bowl. There must be something wrong with your spoon. Now, tell me about my father. Did his blood fall like rain? Does he compost our tulips? Or did he actually make it to war?"

And Mother smiled--because her boy was learning. Soon his mind would be as sharp as hers...and his words would hew.

The next day, Harold dug through his old trunk until he uncovered his first sword--the one he'd discovered in the garden. Underneath it, he found the shield Mother made him from Grandmother's silver charger. He carried them both into the tulip bed, borrowed a shovel from the gardener and--with the ghost standing over his shoulder (who may or may not have been his great uncle or a bastard cousin or even his bloodthirsty soldier father)-- buried the weapons. He didn't need them anymore. In fact, Harold thought he might rather be a diplomat than a soldier. Mayhap, a king.

He replanted the tulip bulbs, brushed the dirt off his palms and headed into the house.

He never saw the ghost again.

When Harold was king, his words did hew. His soldiers did, too. And his Queen, well, she was a bit of a warmonger herself. Lovely woman. Even his mother thought so.

H.L. Fullerton writes fiction—mostly speculative, occasionally about bloodthirsty ghosts and the children that decapitate them—which has been published in more than 60 markets including Tales to Terrify, Kaleidotrope, and Underland Arcana. On Twitter as @ByHLFullerton

Watchlist
Reviews

There's still plenty of genre fiction on our screens, but it's patchy, often with long gaps between series and the recent writers and actors strikes certainly haven't helped. When it's good it's (generally) good, but I long for the days when you'd get a new series of your favourite show every year (and it would be a satisfyingly generous number of episodes long). I saw a twitter thread the other day asking the question (paraphrasing) would you like your new, favourite expensive show to be a lovingly crafted short-run appearing every twelfth of never for $$$$$ per episode, or would you prefer something cheaper that comes out regularly and skimps a bit on the CGI? The comments were surprisingly balanced, but the consensus seemed to be that maybe there's a compromise to be had between auteur excess and a reckless abandonment of deadlines and something more regular that you can get your teeth into.

That seem sensible to me. Great long gaps between series kills momentum, and skimping on episode numbers is irritatingly unsatisfying. I loved the first seasons of *Carnival Row*, *Shadow and Bone* and *Sweet Tooth*, for instance, but in the aeons between releases I found I'd forgotten what it is I liked about the shows in the first place. *Carnival Row* pulled me back, but *Shadow and Bone* season 2 felt distinctly meh and I stopped watching the second outing of *Sweet Tooth* after a couple of episodes. If only season two had come when I still remembered Season one.

And there's the *Stranger Things* problem. How do you explain away the fact that the kids in the first season age at such a rate? There's no story time gap between seasons, but my how they've grown. *Walking Dead's* timeslips get over that problem to a certain extent, but you need some serious audience disbelief when the kids in the stories you love are now being played by twentysomethings. How old is the teenage Spiderman now (I'll save you the Google search – Tom Holland's 27)? If only new seasons and films came out every year, like they used to,

And episode numbers? It feels like shrinkflation, that odious marketing practice where instead of charging more for your Snickers bar the manufacturers just make it a little smaller, hoping you won't notice, or put a couple fewer Quality Street in the tin (if it rattles a bit more, put in some extra packaging). So, Marvel, what's the deal with *Echo*? Only five episodes now? Really? Was it worth all that effort?

Then there's the streamer's tendency to cancel our favourites just when they're beginning to build up momentum. This isn't new – I'm still waiting for *Firefly* to pick up where it impressively left off – but it's increasingly annoying when you only get eight or ten episodes of a series in the first place. The promising *One Piece* on Netflix, for instance: don't hold your breath (cancelled after one season and eight episodes). The acclaimed *Andor*, supposed bright spot of Disney's confused Star Wars roll out strategy? We'll at least it gets a second (and last) season. No more *Doom Patrol*, *Fear the Walking Dead* (though it its defence it did manage eight seasons), *The Flash* (as The CW abandons anything DC) *Gotham*

Knights (1 season), *The Handmaid's Tale*, *Outlander*, *Pennyworth*, *The Peripheral* (after one season, eight highly impressive episodes and a cliffhanger ending), *Snowpiercer* (cancelled after 3 seasons and a cliffhanger, despite a fourth season initially being ordered), *Stranger Things*, *Superman and Lois*, *Titans*, the Umbrella Academy (inexplicably) and one season wonder *The Vampire Academy* (thankfully).

Some of this is about stories reaching their natural end (*Stranger Things*, *The Handmaid's Tale*) and no-one wants to see a fine tale outstay its welcome, but some popular programmes have clearly been cut down mid stride (*Snowpiercer*, *the Peripheral*) and that's deeply unsatisfying. *Snowpiercer* may yet survive – there are rumours that, Expanse-like, it may be picked up by a rival streamer – but for many others, the tale is familiar and depressing. Often expensively produced first seasons lead to long waits for the next and then premature cancellation leaving a distinctly unsatisfying taste in the mouth.

If only the studios could think long term, have a greater understanding of their audience's needs (not just the fan boys) and be a bit more sensible about initially) splashing the cash so the fine programmes that creators aspire to make can have a fighting chance of making sense financially down the line. They have a vested interest in doing just that, but I guess new, shiny baubles are way more tempting than the grind of growing and keeping a dedicated audience. Sigh.

Which all brings me neatly on to Marvel, formerly the golden boy of money-spinning media and now suffering something of a backlash, with some poorly received Disney+ offerings and indifferently performing films. Has the bubble burst, or is it (as Disney Chief and therefore Marvel Big Boss Bob Iger thinks) a case of too much product and audience fatigue?

It's astonishing how much the social media echo chamber has repeated the Iger fatigue view, but it's plainly rubbish. Marvel output has been intermittent at best and positively snail like at worst. Sure, it may be a victim of its own complexity (we'll come on to *Loki* later), but multiple delays (and not just because of strikes), cancellations, downgradings and general faffing around are way more of a problem than any perceived audience overload. Surely we're all desperate for some more Avengers (2026 if we're lucky) the introduction of The Fantastic Four (now

back to 2025) and more X-Men (Deadpool and Wolverine next May, assuming there's still enough time for the reshoots, but nothing planned for the wider cast). The TV series were always meant to fill in the gaps, but in the absence of major film events, they're having to do the heavy lifting too (*Loki* again). But five episodes series' and occasional 'special events' aren't really going to cut it. Overload? It's a desert out here. And when the hell are we going to get *Daredevil?*

Delays and inconsistencies are probably killing the MCU but it's such a juggernaut that Disney would have to be seriously inept for it to go down like Sheild's helicarrier. If only they'd pick a strategy that maximises the potential of their great characters, sticks to the early MCU model of consistent storytelling and subtle interweaving of characters, watch the pennies so that their movies don't have to break all box office records just to break even, get the scripts right in the first place so they don't have to do costly, delaying reshoots and sort out the CGI monster they've created. Objectively, how astonishing does that city's worth of people on the closing credits of any Marvel project look? Does a story really need that many people to work?

I hope that Disney is giving Kevin Feige and his experienced Marvel colleagues the space they need to develop the MCU in the successful they used to, but Feige is getting increasingly distracted (*Star Wars*) and Iger's frequent negative comments about Marvel's strategy seem to suggest that things have changed. I hope not.

Which brings me on to another new Disney toy: *Doctor Who*. *Who*'s not new, of course (the upcoming season will be the 40th, or 14th depending on your point of view) but the link with Disney+ is: wide distribution on one of the world's major streaming services will (hopefully) bring a new and expanded

but we're in safe hands following the return of original and acclaimed showrunner Russell T Davies after the disastrous Chris Chibnall era. Plus, reassuringly, new episodes should come thick and fast in the new year.

Chibnall's *Who* suffered from patchy writing, lengthy delays between seasons

audience to the programme. But the new season (or 'series' in British language. And don't get me started on 'franchise') will be Season One. Which of course, makes zero sense to those of us who grew up cowering behind the sofa as the Daleks laid waste to London.

Will it be any good? First up, confusingly (but gloriously), we've got three long episodes with many people's favourite previous doctor (David Tennant, who left the show in 2010) before we get on to the fifteenth doctor (explain how that can work with your Season One nonsense, Disney). It's a bold choice – *Sex Education*'s Ncuti Gatwa represents a number of firsts for the traditionally white, straight Doctor,

and shrinking episode counts, plus some odd scheduling choices (dumping *Who* to Sundays and dropping the Christmas Special, for instance). Poor Jodie Whittaker never really stood a chance with such poor treatment, but let's hope we see her again in some guise. Another sadly mistreated former doctor was Paul McGann's Eighth Doctor, only seen in one 1996 US/UK TV pilot, a mini episode for the 50th anniversary and a cameo in a Whittaker episode – barely two hours of screen time in total. But Disney money means a spin off with McGann's popular incarnation of the Doctor is a distinct possibility according to the Daily Mirror (who sound like they're more than just guessing).

So things are looking up for *Doctor Who* – I'll report back on all the various upcoming Specials next time – I'm confident we'll all be happy.

Apple TV* is rapidly developing a reputation for consistently putting the best shows out. The excellent *For All Mankind* is currently through its fourth run and is as slick as ever – the basic premise is that the Russians won the space race and landed on the Moon first, Asimov adaptation Foundation has some entertaining visuals but a seemingly random plot, with clone-emperors and secret Foundations, adventure seeking missionaries, a prophet-mother with a daughter who's older than she is (time dilation) and the dead but resurrected Hari Seldon, who's developed an algorithm to predict the future, galaxy wide, for millennia. This adaptation is so far from the source material that, bar the names and the central premise, it's virtually

which supercharged rather than dampened the battle for space supremacy. By Season Four we're in 2003, hoping to form a permanent presence on Mars – 100% approval rating on Rotten Tomatoes so far, so if you haven't picked it up yet, what are you waiting for?

Apple TV seems committed to genre fiction. As well as the Jason Momoa led fantasy series, See, a couple of other shows have just concluded their current runs (thankfully renewed). The patchy unrecognisable, but it's watchable, if occasionally perplexing.

Far better is *Invasion,* with its second run just ended, which is a slow burn weird alien conquest tale following various groups of people as they dodge and weave between battle scenes to seek ways of stopping the aliens polluting large areas and sending hunt and kill robots to carve a bloody trail through the rapidly diminishing population. We've got the *Stranger Things* style teenager group travelling to Paris in search of a boy who can talk to the aliens, the navy SEAL turned maverick, the distressed Japanese scientist looking for her dead lover at the heart of the alien's hive mind and the single-minded ruthless mother who will go to any lengths to protect her children and whose son, and his alien artefact, my just be the key to unravelling the mysteries of the alien menace. It all ends on a cliffhanger, so season Three had better happen, Apple.

Away from Apple, Amazon Prime is currently running a new season of *Upload* (probably finished by the time you read this), the comedy about rich people uploading their minds to a virtual retirement resort, full of dastardly double dealings, improbably (and technically difficult) relationships and some serious social inequalities. Upload covers serious issues in a lighthearted way and is a real gem – clever script, great characters and some great lines.

Amazon is also screening *Gen V*, a spin off from their superhero series *The Boys*, where teens are given a compound that gives them superpowers, which leads,

predictably, to mayhem. Theis world is a cynical look at heroism and justice. It's got a *Titans* vibe, which isn't necessarily a good thing. The Supes are all compromised in one way or another and their world is messily violent – great if you like that sort of thing but like being repeatedly punched in the face if you don't.

Disney+ has just concluded the current run of *Loki*, where the storyline set up in the first season about the Time Variance Authority and its control over the multiverse, threatened by the death of He Who Remains (a variant of Marvel villain Kang the Conqueror) at the hands of Loki variant Sylvie. Confused yet? And that's with me simplifying. By Season two the timelines are unravelling and Loki, Sylvie and Mobius (a TVA employee played by Owen Wilson) try various ways to stick them back together. What follows is well acted, thought provoking, visually interesting and fast paced. It also makes very little sense. Whether it's better than the rest of Marvel's recent Disney+ output depends on your point of view – I think that's been getting an underserved bad press – but it's certainly very watchable, and probably essential viewing if you want to make sense of Marvel's future multiverse movies.

In the near future, watch out for Zack Snyder's *Rebel Moon* (space opera – Dec 22nd), more Hunger Games in *The Ballad of Songbirds and Snakes* (dystopia – Nov 17th), *Godzilla Minus One* (monster mayhem -Dec 1st) and *Orphan Black Echoes* starring Jennifer Jones' Krysten Ritter (already out in Australia – the rest of us should get it soon). Plus all that Doctor Who will hopefully make it feel like it might be a feast after the famine. So plenty for us to talk about next time. Happy watching.

Mark Bilsborough

Bookworm
The Review Team

Conquest
Nina Allan

Maybe, just maybe aliens are already here. And maybe the evidence is in music, in the ground-breaking tonality of Bach, or in an obscure novella about a tower built with

alien, mind altering stone. Or in strange, atypical lichen covering ancient trees which might, just might, bear witness to an alien landing site and the contamination it might have left in its wake.

All is not as it seems in Nina Allan's *Conquest*. There are mysteries, but not just about who might be conquering who, and for what, but on a character level too – a vulnerable adult and genius coder, Frank, gets sucked into conspiracy theories about secret plots, alien infestations and 'n-men', following a rabbit hole set by wealthy, charismatic crime-connected intellectual Eddie de Groote. Frank is persuaded to take a trip to Paris by de Groote but then disappears, to the consternation of his girlfriend, Rachel. In desperation, she employs a private detective with a complex backstory, Robin, who goes in search of Frank. In the process she finds she's searching for understanding of her own past, too, with some surprising revelations.

This novel was written straddling Covid, and the author makes clear in her notes that it changed because of that. There are Covid references and questions raised as to origins, but ultimately I see this book as primarily about relationships, mysteries and understandings. It's got an interesting, creative narrative style that meshes well with the characters and the subject matter but I found the most satisfying part the reproduction of the 'found' 1950s novella (The Tower) that Frank, being Frank, takes as more fact than fiction: a straightforward, linear narrative about a subtle conquest, not with guns and missiles but with the subversion of thought and the infiltration of alien DNA.

Allan's book makes solid ground seem intangible: she asks questions but leaves the answers lingering, even to the extent of providing two alternate endings, neither of them actually addressing the key issues (a strength, not a weakness. She has the good sense to leave things dangling). She writes well, but I suspect it would help to have a good knowledge for classical music to appreciate some of the passages. Both of the key characters – Frank and Robin – love Bach but possibly for different reasons: for Frank, "Bach's music was

not simply music but an alien code",
and for Robin, it's about discovery.

An interesting novel, though it does
have a tendency to wander around the
main plotline and I'm not quite sure it
delivers at the end. That said, it's
engaging, challenging and entertaining
– a caveated recommendation from me.
(*Mark Bilsborough*)

Episode Thirteen
Craig DiLouie

"Episode Thirteen" is an epistolary novel that records the investigations of four characters in Foundation House, a haunted house in Virginia. They are there to film the final episode of Fade to Black, a TV show about ghost hunting. "Episode Thirteen" is very fast-paced. I finished it in three days, but I can see someone else finishing it in a day or two. One reason for its briskness is its use of blank space. The shortest journal entry is just two sentences long, leaving the rest of the page empty. The absence of words is especially noticeable in the text conversations between one of the investigators, Jessica, and her sister. These conversations are presented as alternating speech bubbles, like in a messaging app. In both the journal entries and the conversations, the prevalence of blank space suggests shock, uncertainty, and a blankness of mind. It also represents a blank slate on which to form our own conclusions about the characters, recalling the Editor's Note at the start of the novel, which invites the reader to "make up your own mind whether to believe".

My favourite instance of ambiguity is the email from Ramsay, a physics professor, to Claire, his former student and one of the investigators. He emails her in response to a request for his help, writing in such a way that we cannot be sure if he is mocking her. One paragraph reads: "I hope they are compensating you handsomely for the Sisyphean task of knocking down pseudoscience every week. Otherwise, one might consider it unworthy of your extraordinary talent and intellect. Of course, I intend that to be taken as flattery instead of criticism." Apart from this email, Ramsay does not make an appearance in the story; his words are our only means of understanding his attitude towards Claire. We are alerted to the inadequacy of the data given to us, which seems to contradict the editor's goal of letting us make our own judgements. But maybe the editor's point is precisely that nothing can really be known. Indeed, even the journal entries of the investigators, which presumably reveal their "true" opinions, may not be objective because they are not written voluntarily, but at the bidding of the chief investigator, Matt. As a result, the other investigators are always writing with the awareness that he might confiscate their journals in future, discouraging them from sharing their innermost thoughts.

I found the interpersonal conflicts intriguing and I wish they had played a larger role in the story. In particular, the scene in which the investigators discover documents exposing their darkest secrets seems to signal a turning point, foreshadowing a climax involving back-to-back betrayal. The actual climax, however, positions the investigators not against one another, but against an external evil, causing the tensions within the group to be swept under the rug in a somewhat unsatisfying way. Still, the irresistible premise of "Episode Thirteen" snatched my attention, forcing me to read it in its entirety. *(Ryan Tan)*

Lords of Uncreation
Adrian Tchaikovsky

Lords of Uncreation is the concluding novel in prolific author and recent BSFA award winner Adrian Tchaikovsky's *Final Architecture* trilogy (after *Shards of Earth* and *Eyes of the Void*) – a space opera on a galactic scale with alien threats, weird science and extensive, book-spanning action sequences. It's a pacy, unrelenting, driving narrative with quirky, engaging all-action heroes and malevolent, brooding bad guys. In other words, it takes a formula, distils it to its essence and runs with it. Don't come to this one looking for subtlety or nuance – but it does what it does well, and I'm sure the film rights have been snapped up already.

As is the way with this type of novel, the stakes are high. Set in the mid-distant future, many of the inhabited planets across the galaxy have been reshaped into sculptures by a mysterious and uncommunicative set of ancient aliens known as the Architects, who appear out of 'unspace' (a kind of wormhole) forcing populations to flee as their worlds become uninhabitable. Earth is one of the planets destroyed by the Architects and humanity (as well as many other species) survives in small, easily moveable colonies on hidden worlds and on large 'Ark' ships.

Previous novels established that some people – Ints (intermediaries) – can sense the Architects and predict their arrival – and in some cases can partially communicate with them, occasionally persuading them to return to Unspace. There is speculation that something greater and more malevolent lies behind the Architects, and the key to ending the conflict is tracking them down.

The protagonists are primarily the crew and associates of the Vulture God, a salvage ship, and include one of the more skilled Ints, Idris Telemmier, a disabled but exo-skeleton enhanced engineer Olli, alien archaeologist Trine, and an enhanced human, Solace, from a female led breakaway human faction, the Partheni, The many and varied antagonists include a megalomaniac, ruthless nobleman Ravin and an alien slave owner and despot The Unspeakable Aklu (a leading member of the international crime syndicate-cum-empire the Hegmony) The cast is much larger than this, but listed in full reads

like the credits after a Marvel movie –
fortunately there's a glossary!

Events leading up to this final
instalment in the trilogy include the
discovery of a massive alien artefact
called the Eye, which harnessed with
other tech has the ability to track
Architect movements in Unspace and
gives hope that an attack through
Unspace can end the conflict. But
control of the Eye is disputed - and the
uneasy alliance between natural
enemies, alien and human, is fractious
and unstable.

Lords of Uncreation begins with a
forcibly modified slave Int, Andecka,
confronting an Architect about to
destroy a planet, which gives us a feel
for the scale of the conflict. We then shift
to a spaceship surrounding the Eye,
which has Ints (including Idris) looking
out into Unspace and a different
perspective on the conflict, leading to
arguments over strategy. With the Eye
now critical to survival in the constantly
battered galaxy, its importance leads to
shifting alliances, and the inevitable
conflict that brings.

These novels are firmly into Alastair
Reynolds, Peter F Hamilton and Gareth
Powell territory, with a broad spread of
characters, plenty of tension and
existential threats, but I found them
difficult to follow at times, possibly
because of the sheer size of the novels
(this third instalment comes in at just
under 600 pages), the number of
characters, shifts in point of view and
the emphasis on action rather than
characterisation.   Nevertheless,
Tchaikovsky   has   once   again
demonstrated her that he's at the peak
of his award-winning powers, and this
book delivers. *(Mark Bilsborough)*

The Unit
Ninni Holmqvist

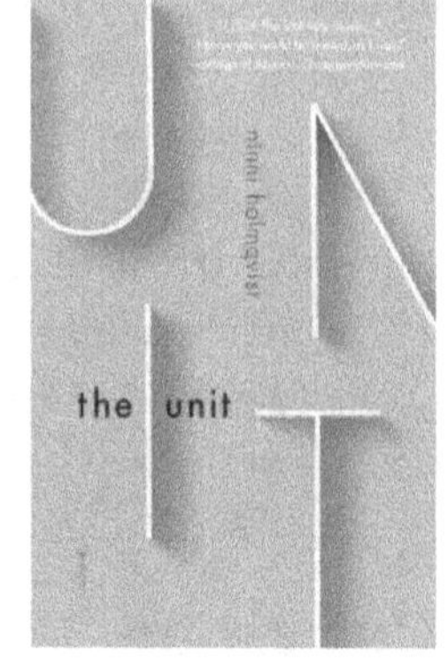

Imagine a world
where 50-year-
old women and
60-year-old men
who are childless
and without a
useful career are
classed as
'dispensable' and
sent to live out
their days in a special unit. Troubling?
Chilling? Well, sit back and prepare to
be absorbed as this is the world that
Ninni Holmqvist has created in her
moving, speculative fiction novel.

'The Unit' is a story of acceptance, loss
and friendship. The protagonist, 'Dorrit'
calmly resigns herself to her fate. The
good news is that her life as a
dispensable in The Unit will be one of
luxury: her own plush apartment,
beautiful gardens, spa facilities, leisure
activities. The bad news is that she will
have to take part in clinical trials,
provide organ donations and eventually
make a 'final donation' which will lead
to her death.

There is more than a tinge of Ishiguro's
'Never Let Me Go' in this story.
However, the difference here is that the
donors are older adults, and they know
exactly what is going to happen to them.
Before entering The Unit, Dorrit had
been a moderately successful writer, but
writers are not seen as economically
necessary in this world. In fact, she is

told that: "People who read books… tend to be dispensable. Extremely". She enters a place where lavish comfort goes hand in hand with constant surveillance. For the first time in her life, she makes close friendships, yet all relationships in The Unit have a bittersweet inevitability. Conflict arises and things become poignantly complicated when she meets a man and falls in love.

Translated from Swedish in 2009 and re-issued recently, the tone of this debut novel is matter of fact in its depiction of a society where quiet cruelty is the norm. The prose is plain yet beautiful, cleverly avoiding any sense of self-pity and making us question the definition of 'worth' in our society. In Holmqvist's near-future world, not being needed by anyone might seem advantageous for the young, but it's a lifestyle that will prove a death sentence in middle age. *(Sandraa Baker)*

Paradise-1
David Wellington

Endless Dark, Endless Terror, the cover blurb promises, and with this novel weighing in at over 600 pages, I was certainly expecting the endless part. What I wasn't expecting was turning to the last page quite so quickly – because this is a novel that won't let up. There's hardly a page goes by that that the pace slackens and when it does, there's some other massive problem right around the corner.

A hugely enjoyable (if sometimes disturbing) sci-fi horror tale of a small spacecraft sent to a colony planet to check in on the colonists who've gone strangely silent. The planet in question is Paradise 1, and with a name like that it's clearly asking or trouble, right? On board are 'Firewatch' agent Sasha Petrova, failed pilot Sam Parker, neurotic doctor Zhang Lei and a robot with attitude called Rasputin. A classic misfits in trouble unit. They become a tight, well developed team that will no doubt see us through many a sequel, and they're full of mysteries and secrets.

When the ship gets to Paradise they find that the place is guarded by over a hundred Earth ships and they can't get to the surface. Worse, their ship's AI has gone into emergency shutdown and is constantly rebooting itself, leaving them almost helpless. And even worse, the other ships in orbit are trying to kill them.

The dialogue is snappy and the characters are engaging with a narrative that screams 'action thriller'. It's not particularly original (though the principle antagonist is scarily different) but that doesn't matter when the writing is as immersive as this. In the right hands, this would make a great movie.

I wasn't bowled over by the big reveals but the strengths of this type of book are all in the journey, not the destination. And the sequel is very nicely set up. *(Mark Bilsborough)*